The

Alp

Arno

Camenisch

The

Alp

a novel, translated by Donal McLaughlin

DALKEY ARCHIVE PRESS
Champaign / London / Dublin

Originally published in Rhaeto-Romanic and German
as *Sez Ner* by Urs Engeler, Basel in 2009

Camenisch, Arno, 1978- author.
    [Sez Ner. English]
    The Alp / Arno Camenisch ; translated by Donal McLaughlin. --
First Edition.
        pages cm
    ISBN 978-1-62897-010-4 (pbk. : acid-free paper)
    I. McLaughlin, Donal, 1961- translator. II. Title.
    PT2703.A57S4913 2014
    833'.92--dc23
                                    2014001111

Donal McLaughlin acknowledges, with gratitude, the receipt
of a grant from the Max Geilinger Foundation in 2013.

ILLINOIS
ARTS
COUNCIL
AGENCY

swiss arts council
prɔhelvetia

This publication is partially funded by a grant from the Illinois Arts Council,
a state agency, and the Swiss Arts Council Pro Helvetia

ART WORKS. | National
Endowment
for the Arts
arts.gov

This publication is supported in part by an award
from the National Endowment for the Arts.

www.dalkeyarchive.com

Cover: design and composition by Mikhail Iliatov
Printed on permanent/durable and acid-free paper

The
Alp

THE DAIRYMAN'S HANGING FROM A PARAGLIDER, in the red firs
below the hut on the alp at the foot of Sez Ner. You can hear
him cursing from the hut. He has his back to the mountain, is
facing the range across the valley where, shoulder to shoulder,
peak after peak rises, Piz Tumpiv at the center, all 3,101 meters
of it, that amazing presence it has, outdoing the other—snow-
less—peaks. He'll come down when he's ready, his farmhand
says. Let him wriggle for another while. That'll teach him not
to clear the trees.

The cheese is swelling. During the night, the stone weights crash
to the floor, wakening everyone. The swineherd and the cowherd carry the over-ripened cheeses through the clear night,
across the yard, through the cowshed, to behind the cowshed,
and dump them in the slurry. Neither the dairyman nor his
farmhand budges to help. They stay where they are in the doorway, their hands in their pockets.

The farmhand has eight fingers, five on his left hand, and three
on his right. His right he keeps mostly in his pocket, or resting
on his thigh beneath the table. When he lies in the grass outside the hut, next to the pigpen, fast asleep with his boots off,
and socks off as well, the swineherd counts his toes. The farmhand sleeps in the afternoons as, by night, he's out and about.
He vanishes when everyone's gone to bed, comes back at some
point during the night. He takes the dogs, to stop them barking.

The swineherd has a bad conscience. A pig's lying in the pen and won't get up. Its cold snout, the swineherd knows, means the pig's a goner, but he pokes the lump of ham with his steel-toed boots anyway. It could still get up, sure. *Quel ei futsch, ti tgutg,* the dairyman says. Just nineteen pigs now. Twenty, counting you, the swineherd thinks. The dairyman returns to the cowshed, his one-legged milking stool around his waist, and the swineherd takes the pigs back up to the pigsty, willing that stool to collapse. In the pigsty, he counts the pigs, makes it eighteen standing and one lying down. That one's a goner, too. That's how swift it can be, the swineherd thinks. Keep going at this rate, and there'll be none left in the morning and I can take myself home. The evening sun's already sinking behind the mountains, Piz Tumpiv dark yellow in the dusk, when the vet arrives—that guy Tscharner with his beard, fat stomach and fat son—who doesn't acknowledge the swineherd, just the dairyman. They've eaten too much, the vet says to the dairyman, their insides have burst.

Clemens's cow, the dark one, head-butts the fencepost, knocking it over. Clemens's cow gets out, and his other five cows trot after her. The vet says cows are bright, much brighter than horses. With horses it's all about status, he says. They might look elegant but, basically, they're dumb. Cows may well be more intelligent. Right now though, the cowherd's scouring the forest, hoping to find Clemens's cows before the sun goes right down.

Later in the evening, the cowherd from the alp bordering with Stavonas comes by in the car. She's just back from Glion, apparently, where she had her dog neutered. It all went smoothly, it seems, but the thing's totally dazed, still. She opens the rear door of the red car—where the dog's been allowed to lie this once. Whimpering and whining, it is. He doesn't seem to want out, she says, and the dog just lies where it is. It'll be fine, the farmhand says. Takes a bit of time, that's all. The cowherd says to come with her, to help her carry the dog from the car, up on the alp. The farmhand does so, takes his own dogs too. They run along behind, there's no space in the car. He whistles out the window to make them keep up. Make sure they don't turn back.

In the morning, on the bench outside the hut, the dairyman's out for the count with a half-empty bottle of schnapps in his hand, while the goat's up on the divan, up in his room, admiring the view of Tumpiv, maybe; peeing on the bed, for sure.

Every day, the pigs get out of their pen, down from the hut. They dig beneath the electric fence and head across the pastures, down to the trees where the dairyman was hanging. The swineherd doesn't care, knows—come the evening—they'll be back. The dairyman does care. Show them who's boss, he says, thrusting the rod with the rings into the swineherd's hand, and packing the farmhand off with him. In the pigsty, the farmhand takes the rod and the rings, and the swineherd picks a pig, grabs it by the ears, and jumps on its back, making it squeal even louder. He pulls its ears back and digs his knees into its ribs, to help the farmhand get the rod in its nose, and press. Once the ring is on, the pig bolts to the opposite corner, to hide behind the other pigs, who lick the blood from its snout.

Tourists arrive on the dirt road, improved last spring, stop their beautiful cars at the fence outside the hut and toot the horn. Seeing Cowherd and Swineherd sprawled on the grass on the slope above the hut, they toot again. They keep tooting until—finally—they give up, get out of their beautiful cars, open the gate themselves, and drive on. Twenty minutes later, they're reversing back down as the road doesn't go much further and hasn't a big enough turning space. They have to stop at the gate again, the gate they left open but is now shut again, to reopen it. This time, the two herders, sprawling on the grass still, wave to them.

You hear him before you see him: the priest rounds the corner on his moped, sending dust flying everywhere. He's wearing a helmet in the afternoon sun, and his cassock flutters in the wind he's creating. Seeing this, the dogs bark and leap at the priest, send him spinning down the slope, nearly, into the alpenroses. The priest parks his moped beside the hut and is given a coffee before he asks them all to gather in front of the hut that looks onto the mountains, gives the dog jumping up and licking him a slap, then invites them all to pray to God Almighty, Lord of all they see before them, for the summer they've not yet had. A wind comes up, and the herd moves down in front of the cowshed as the priest, now with a stole round his neck, hands out prayer books from among the cows and beasts. He announces which page it is, then reads it to them. The pigs have got out too, and come up to the priest and snatch at his cassock. The herdsmen on the alp repeat whatever the priest says, like parrots. A good half hour it is before the final *Amen*, before everything's been blessed that needed blessing and, a wheel of cheese and five kilos of butter richer, the priest gets back on his moped, pushes his way through the waiting, already grumpy herd, and—in the last of the light—vanishes.

The black ram with the white patch on its head is bang in the middle of the cowshed when the cows come crashing in and break its legs. Both front legs end up in plaster. The black ram is anything but tame. Normally, he wouldn't let you pet him. In plaster, he does: he can't get away. One time before, when he was tied to the cowshed—his legs, at that point, were still in one piece—he snapped the rope in two when the swineherd tried to go up to him, and ran away. There's no need to be afraid of the swineherd, the farmhand says.

The rooster isn't afraid, it doesn't run away, is one aggressive bastard, the farmhand says. When the farmhand gets too close, it jumps up at him. Your man's steel-toed boots it takes, to shoo it away. The rooster, a handsome beast, guards its hens, covers them constantly. Any time, any place, anywhere.

Kneeling at his bed, the cowherd shows the swineherd the projectiles he found among the edelweiss and alpenroses. The length of your lower arm, the projectiles are, all twisted and bent, some with, some without heads. The swineherd turns them all the way around, throws them in the air, and catches them. They end up back under the bed, with the cloth over them. On one occasion, when the dairyman—for once—goes into the pastures, he finds a projectile too. He orders the two herders to put a fence up around it right away, a good distance away, then puts the cowherd on sentry duty, and drives down to the village in his Subaru Justy. Early that afternoon, a military convoy rounds the corner, three huge vehicles with specialists in them, wearing gloves and special uniforms. They're careful not to touch the projectile, crawl up to it from different angles, have instruments they note down readings from. Finally, they dispose of the projectile and walk, in step, back down the pasture to outside the hut again, the officer out in front. Not a word is spoken as they climb into the camouflage vehicles. And disappear, in a cloud of dust.

The dog's jumping up and licking the cowherd, the other dog, the older one, is trotting ahead, in front. The young dog jumps and sinks its teeth in the cows' tails, gets a free ride until the cow hits it a kick and the dog, with a whimper, lets go. Its tail between its legs, it gives the cows a wide berth on its way back to its master. They get on well, the young dog and the old gray one. They only ever fight over food.

The one with the limp doesn't want to move, the one with the limp trots behind the others, stopping time and again. The cowherd takes his stick to her, beats her on the back till the stick breaks. The herd has vanished, long since, into the trees.

Late in the evening, at the side of the hut, the dairyman's at the wheel of his gray Subaru Justy, the bottle of plum brandy in his hand. His farmhand's beside him, in the passenger seat. The cowherd and the swineherd and the dogs are behind him, in the back. The car's the safest place to be, the dairyman says. Each time the lightning strikes, ruins the cowherd's fences, or sets the firs at the edge of the forest alight, he winces. The rain sweeps across the alp, giving both it and the filthy Subaru a good clean.

In the side valley, on the other side of the valley, the wall of the dam between the wooded slopes seals the valley. On the wall of the dam, someone's hanging on ropes, an ertist, the farmers said, an ertist painting the wall up nice, in remembrance of General Suvorov. He's painted figures on the left, and blue and white squares. Black figures with big hats, striding across the wall of the dam where the sun draws its shadow border. The farmhand offers the swineherd the binoculars so he can see the ertist hanging. The swineherd sees the broad green valley beyond the wall.

The young dog—its dick's stiff—is sitting beside the swineherd. It's wagging its tail and its tongue's hanging out. It lifts its paw and scratches the swineherd's thigh until the swineherd pats its head, scratches behind its ears and strokes its ribs. He puts the binoculars down. Down from the hut, at the tree line, the herd of pigs is moving along the edge of the forest. He can hear the pigs squeal. They keep their snouts just above the ground, their ears hanging forward like blinkers.

The farmers come on Sundays when they come. They stand between the hut and the pigpen, with their hands in their pockets and Brissago cigars poking out of their beards, as they watch the herd go in. When there are visitors around, the farmhand whistles to the cowherd and the swineherd, who follow behind the herd, so they know they have company, and to go easy with the sticks.

The farmers go through the cowshed. They stroke the cows' steaming backs, feel their udders, nod, stroke the back of the cows' necks, nod, then toast his good work with the dairyman.

Outside the cowshed, the swineherd removes the full churn from the milking machine, his right hand gripping the bottom. The dirty edge of the churn bites into his finger joints. The milk foams in the red pails, splashes over the rims and onto his black steel-toed boots. The young dog licks the milk from the steel-toe.

Can he take a few wheels of cheese home with him, the farmer asks, after drinking a toast with the dairyman, shaking hands with the farmhand, patting the cowherd on the shoulder, and nodding to the swineherd. He'd be happy to.

The swineherd trips over a slab in the yard and lands on his belly in the shit. The full pails hurtle through the air and the milk spills across the yard, through the cow shit, into the cracks between the slabs. The milk turns brownish. His skinned knuckles sting, his chin, too. The swineherd wishes he could lie there until summer's over.

During the night, the cow scratches against the hut. It scratches its neck against the corner, moves its head back and forth, shakes its head, rubs its head up and down the edge, its cowbell ringing all the while. The dairyman gets up during the night, stands in his underpants at the window—where, by day, he can see Piz Tumpiv, by night, can only guess where it is—and screams. The cow continues to scratch against the corner till the dairyman appears in the doorway in his underpants and boots and connects with the stick he's wielding between the cow's horns, then thumps it another time, on the nose, another time on the back, then kicks it in the stomach. When the cow's gone, the dairyman slams the door.

The sun gradually warms the humid, clear air and the last scraps of white cloud vanish. The swineherd removes the cowpats from the yard with the manure shovel and tips them into the wheelbarrow. The wheelbarrow has a handle missing and its flat tire squeaks.

As he sweeps the yard with the broom from the cowshed, the swineherd counts the slabs. When he has swept the whole yard, he knows no more than the day before: the yard has 711 slabs. Of which 51 are cracked, 12 are in four bits, and 22 have a corner chipped off.

Toni Liung's cow, the light-colored one, has torn its right horn off. The blood's sticking to the stump of the horn, the blood's sticking to the cow's ear, its neck, its right cheek. A swarm of flies is buzzing round its head. It shakes its head and the flies fly off, then land again to eat their fill of fresh blood.

The black ram limps across the yard with its front legs in dirty plaster casts. It has lost weight, you can feel its ribs, the farmhand says with his cup in his left hand. The farmhand looks after the ram. The ram doesn't defy him. The ram hasn't been back in the cowshed and is rarely known to limp across the yard. When the ram notices the swineherd up at the fountain, it does an about-turn and goes under the fence.

The farmer's behind the hut, stroking Marta's ribs and patting her cheek. Marta sticks her tongue out, reaches for the farmer's sleeve. The farmer's proud grin is as broad as a barn door. Is that Vicki or Otto, the swineherd asks the cowherd, it's easier to tell fence posts apart than those two beards.

The dairyman's at the stove, stirring the rice. To go with it, there's old cheese, already cut, down in the cellar, on the right. The old cheese has a greasy rind, is strong, and full of maggots. You can cut them out, the farmhand says, what doesn't kill you, the dairyman says, will fatten you up.

In winter, two Dutchmen had the idea of sleeping on Sez Ner, the farmer with the bulbous nose says. His Brissago shifts from side to side in his beard, and he nods when the dairyman talks him into another schnapps. He watches the dairyman pour it, then lifts the glass and downs it in one, great for warming you up, that is. They put their tents up, the heathens, probably thinking that's what what's called the romance of the mountains is, winter on Sez Ner. The dairyman nods, seems they nearly froze to death. He shakes his head. The dairyman nods, clamps his Brissago between his forefinger and middle finger. One for the road, he says, knocking the schnapps back, *basta, tgauadia*.

The cowherd cuts some old cheese, eyeing the fresh stuff beside it. Potatoes aren't something the dairyman makes, just *rösti* out of a packet, with fried eggs or pasta. Vegetables aren't something he cooks either, but he does make polenta, polenta and cheese, that'll build you up, he says to the swineherd.

The cowherd and the swineherd are on their feet behind the cowshed, to see which of them can pee the furthest. The cowherd's goes further than the swineherd's, his stream shining in the midday sun. The swineherd says it's precision that counts, more difficult, that is. Go ahead and try, try and hit the head of that rose. The cowherd has too little pee left.

The tabby comes creeping around the corner. The tabby stops at the legs of the herders and brushes against their boots. The tabby belongs to the farmhand. The farmhand has promised the cowherd can take the tabby home at the end of the summer. The swineherd tells the cowherd they should compete for the tabby the next time they have a peeing contest.

In a corner of the hay barn, among the yellowed magazines, the farmhand finds a book, a Calender Romontsch from the Sixties. The book's covered in dust. He wipes away the cobwebs, sits down in the hayloft and flicks through the adverts at the back. *Bonvin toujours, à votre santé.* French, the farmhand can't speak. Coiffeur Franz Kaiser is advertising *cigarras en gros.* Knikos in Chur are pushing *costums da teater.* Kernbeisser-Crocnoisettes by Grison. Androgal, 300 dragées for 47.50. Meat, fresh and dried, from Disentis. Ladies' clothing from Götzer in Chur. Condor Cycles. Alfa-Laval milking machines, 100 *novs models.*

The swineherd is lying awake. The cowherd's asleep and grinding his teeth. In the distance, the swineherd can hear the cowbells from the night pasture, can hear the bell of the goat running around outside the cowshed, can hear the water in the fountain outside the hut. In the room next door, the dairyman is snoring. The swineherd hears the back door of the hut opening, creaking and clicking shut again. He hears footsteps on the wooden floor.

The sun casts the shadow of the photographer from tourist information onto the dirty slabs outside the hut. The flies buzz around his fisherman's hat. The hut door opens and in the doorway stands the dairyman in his flowery herdsman's shirt, with his red cheeks and red socks and red laces in his boots. His boots are shining with milking grease. The magnificent head of hair beneath his decorated hat is dripping. He wipes his hand on the seat of his trousers and offers it to the photographer with the camera bags around his neck, and a tripod. With a well-aimed kick, the dairyman chases the goat down from the wooden bench with the engraved plaque outside the hut, then calls the farmhand. The farmhand appears in the doorway with the cheese knife in his hand. His hands are full so he can't come, he says, and the two herders are off somewhere. The two herders, in their overalls, are lying on their stomachs on the hill above the hut and can hear the dairyman running around the hut and cowshed, cursing them, while alongside the tripod, now set up, complete with camera, its fat lens focused on the mountain backdrop, the photographer unfolds the tourist information leaflet on alpine costumes.

The evening sun is low in the sky. The wind's blowing down the valley, and bending the treetops. From the forest, you can hear the herd approaching. The dogs are barking. The upper part of the Surselva valley is covered in dark clouds. You can hear the storm working its way along the valley, taking village after village, alp after alp. The sun's no longer able to hold its ground, storm clouds darken the alp. The chickens have made themselves scarce and the first raindrops fall. There's lightning and thunder. The dairyman stands in the doorway with his hands in his pockets, beneath his apron, counting the number of seconds between the lightning and the thunder.

In the parlor, beside the radio with the bent aerial on the dresser, is the small bottle of holy water the priest gave to the herdsmen. The small plastic bottle has a blue screw cap. The swineherd screws the cap off and drinks the entire contents.

The dairyman and his farmhand sit on the milking stools they've tied around their waists with their heads against the cows' stomachs and their backs bent beneath the cows, like it was gold they were washing. From the speakers in the cowshed, music is playing. The dairyman says the cows give more milk if music's playing while they're milked. He gets up in between times, gives his back a good stretch, it's been proved—that. The dairyman curses every time a cow tail slaps him on the ear. Every time a tail wasn't tied to the ropes properly. It's worse when the tails have just been trailing in the waste drain.

The swineherd is rubbing shampoo into the heels of his socks. He pours water over them, then rubs his heels till they foam, before putting his boots on. The boots still pinch, to begin with.

The day-trippers wash off their walking boots in the fountain outside the hut. They take their shoes off, and their sweaty socks. The day-trippers sit at the edge of the fountain with their feet in the basin. They dip the dirty soles of their shoes in the water, use their fingers to dig the dirt out of the sole. Thanks a lot, they say when the swineherd brings them a cup of milk, no worries, don't mention it, the swineherd says. That's for the dirt in the fountain, he thinks to himself.

The cows have names, the pigs don't. The pigs are pigs. The cows have round aluminum discs on their ears, and numbers on their rumps. The two herders know each cow by name. They're family as soon as they've a name, the cowherd says to the swineherd in the evening behind the cowshed when the cows are on the night pasture, handing him the Brissago he took from the farmers on Sunday. A cow's not just a cow. The swineherd takes a puff of the Brissago and says he feels sorry for farmers who tell you they've five cows instead of saying, I have Marta, Barla, Marlis, Nicki, and Petra. He coughs, sounds better put like that, doesn't it, and blows the smoke into the night sky. The priest should've blessed the cows individually, by name, and not left it at just blessing the group, the cowherd says, with his hands in his pockets and shifting his Brissago to and fro, between his teeth. If he had, every last beast with a cloven hoof below Sez Ner would be on the right path. The swineherd nods. The silhouettes of the herders behind the cowshed fade in the dark.

The bread's so hard, you could strike a chicken dead with it. The farmhand dips the buttered bread in his coffee. In the cupboard are another two hard loaves, with mold on the crusts, and Thursday's still three days away. The farmhand's always pleased when he can give the goat the hard bread. The goat is pleased too.

The cowherd carries his fork in the trouser pocket of his blue overalls. When he sits down at the table, he takes his fork out of the pocket. He only ever eats with this old fork. Your ass, the dairyman says, it's not as if you couldn't eat with the other forks. Someone should knock that out of you, just wait, I'll bend and twist it every which way, then we'll see you eating with this one, 'cause you won't have any other. At the end of the meal, the cowherd wipes the fork on his trousers and puts it back in his pocket.

Cow horns aren't modern anymore, the farmer says, young farmers wouldn't stand for horns, the stupid asses. He takes his hat in his right hand and wipes his brow with the palm of his left, a cow with no horns isn't a cow at all, and that's that.

The milk inspector hums to himself as he fills milk samples from the cows into his little plastic bottles and notes the milk yields in his book. When he's alone in the hut, he sings hymns in minor and goes back to humming if one of the herders turns up in the doorway with milk pails. The milk inspector doesn't check what the two herders tell him. He couldn't care less how much they attribute to which cow.

41 cows have no horns, 32 have horns, 9 have big horns, 7 have small horns, 3 have stumps of horns and 2 are unicorns.

The petrol-soaked sawdust in the metal bucket behind the big stove is on fire. The flames hiss up the wooden wall, reaching the ceiling almost, while the cowherd, with his spoon in his hand, watches the wood crackling in the big stove. *Pil giavel*, the farm-hand curses, as he comes out of the parlor, with his milking stool still around his waist. When the swineherd turns up in the door-way with two full pails of milk, the farmhand, with his steel-toed boot, kicks the metal bucket out past him. He goes out after it, the flames spitting from the bucket, until the burning bucket comes to a stop where the scraps for the chickens are, be-low the yard, and burns itself out.

The swineherd is in the parlor with the pencil in his hand, not-ing the size of the herd this summer on the inside of the cup-board door. The pencil scratches on the wood. The swineherd can't remember whether the plural of sheep is sheep or sheeps. It's one creep, two creeps, that he does know, so he writes down sheeps, with an s, but something makes him score it out and write in sheep, sheep without an s—at the end, that is—above it. He's still not sure.

On the front cover of the book is a picture of a woman in a head-scarf, bending so far down that her back hurts. In the background is the monastery in Disentis. The first pages are the calendar. The names of the saints have been entered in the cal-endar. In addition to that: on 16 July, the dog days begin; on 9

July at 12.31, windy and fresh; on 23 August at 06.26, rain; on 14 August at 14.13, very hot; on 28 August, the dog days come to an end. On the right-hand pages, is all the advice. If someone answers before he has fully understood a question, he's seen as dull. Blows on the back of a heathen are blows on the back of a nincompoop. The farmhand looks up to the hills where the noses of the first cows are appearing. He can hear the dogs barking.

The pan is shining. The leftovers are lying on the drain beside the cheese kettle. The outside of the pan has been blackened by the fire. The swineherd's glad he has the wire wool. It's just that he can't stand the sound, when the wire wool rubs against the pan. It makes his skin crawl like when his teeth bite into the fork.

The young dog still has a lot to learn, the dairyman says. His farmhand's standing beside him, smoking a Select. He can't see this dope getting as far as the old gray dog—too totally stupid, the young dog is for that. He stands outside the hut in his apron, his eyes following the herders and the herd. The sky has opened up, the clouds have dispersed. With a dog that's worth little to nothing, there's no point in trying to work an alp. Without a dog you're up shit creek, he spits on the ground, and with a dog like this one, you sure as hell are. He wipes his mouth with the back of his hand. The herd has vanished behind the hills, the herders' toes in the swirling dust, too. The old gray one, I trained it, as you can see. The dairyman takes a few steps to the edge of the yard, faces Tumpiv, pushes the apron aside, and unzips his flies. As for that other dope, he doesn't know why he even brought it up with him, fuckin mutt. The farmhand throws the cigarette beyond the yard and into the mud. He strokes the fur of the tabby on the window ledge, ties his apron round him, and goes back into the hut.

Amerika is in the yard, and drinking from the full fountain. Her bell has a dent in it and doesn't have a clapper. She drinks more than the milk she produces, her, the farmhand says.

The dairyman says the one with the limp isn't to go with the herd. The one with the limp stays chained up until the herd and the dogs and the cowherd have gone. Then the farmhand unchains the one with the limp. He strokes her nose. The rough tongue of the one with the limp reaches for the farmhand's sleeve.

In the morning cold and drizzling rain, the cowherd hurries to the night pasture, he has the dog chase around the pasture, *dai, dai,* whistling to urge it forward, while he turns off the Zaunkönig and opens the wire fence. It is still dark at the pasture. The swineherd gets the cows up on their feet, the first go past the Zaunkönig, where the cowherd's waiting, counting the days. Clemens's cows are there too.

The egg has two yolks. The swineherd stirs the yolks in the frying pan. The two yolks mingle even before the egg white turns white in the pan over the heat. The egg now looks like any other.

The dairyman's at the pigpen, looking down to the edge of the forest where, in the afternoon sun, the two herders are running around with buckets, pulling thistles out. He's told them to pull them out at the root, and not to cut them off. The cows don't eat that shit, he said, you now have a good two hours, you two, before they have to be fetched back. On the pastures at the edge of the forest, the herders run around with their buckets and gloves. The dairyman's up at the pigpen, looking down. For as long as the dairyman stays there, the herders pull the thistles out and put them in the buckets.

The ant trail leads across the wooden floor. The ants climb up the parlor table and across it. The ant trail ends at the sugar. The tabby's up on the table and its ears are pricked. Its whiskers are long for a tomcat, stick out like antennae. The tabby drags its paw through the ant trail. It moves its tail to and fro.

They have it good these days, one of the farmers says when the cowherd leaves the parlor. Things were different in the past, he pours them more, he knows of an alp where a herder was castrated. The farmers turn their heads round to the one talking beneath the crucifix. Just the one ball though, he says, stirring his coffee, two bricks, snip, and bye-bye ball. Still running around he is today, with one ball. There was no comparison with the Alps nowadays, holiday camps they were now, compared to before. The cowherd returns to the smoky parlor with a full pot of coffee, that's the way things had been. Discipline them. That way, you wouldn't get so much of their crap all the time. He holds his empty cup out to the cowherd.

The cold water in the morning cold breaks the skin on the herdsmen's hands. Hands like sandpaper. Creams ease it in the afternoon. Next morning, the cold breaks the skin again. The skin breaks at the knuckles first, then at the joints, on the palms. The herdsmen rub in milking grease, that doesn't help either. The only thing that helps any way at all is a stick of ointment, Tuc, 30g, with the screwcap covered in muck. The only thing that really helps is putting your hands in your pockets.

The swineherd's standing on the hill, talking to the cairn. The Stone Man.

The Canadian has a red beard and a wart on his forehead. He's sitting at the edge of the fountain, stroking the tabby's stripes.

He's brought the farmhand fresh bread and a box of cigars, Canadian imports from Maria La Gorda in Cuba. He's flying back in a week, he tells the farmhand, who is sitting beside him at the edge of the fountain. Will he be away for long, the farmhand asks, we'll see. Come and visit me when you're done with all of this, over there the horizon hangs lower, scratching his beard. The farmhand moves his hand to and fro in the water. The tabby jumps down from the edge of the fountain. It runs across the yard and past the cowshed.

There's a button in the soup. It's lying at the bottom of the bowl. The button looks like a coin. Why you not eating, the dairyman asks, ladling a second bowl from the pot on the table, not good enough for a herder, I take it. The swineherd stirs his soup. The button on the sleeve of the dairyman's milking coat is missing.

Among the cows being herded across the hills and down toward the cowshed is the bull from Alp Prada. You can spot it from a distance already. Its shoulder height is way above that of the cows. The cowherd, behind the herd, keeps an eye on the bull. One of Georg's cows is in heat, as was clear this morning before the cows headed up to Sez Ner. She mounted the other cows, pressed her udder against their back legs, behaved as if the world was about to end. The bull broke through the fences on the upper pastures and got in among the herd. The bull knows what he wants.

The tabby's sitting right at the front of the roof of the hut, looking down onto the herd, as it edges its way across the yard. In the distance, church bells are ringing. The herders are herding the cows into the night pasture. The sun's sinking slowly behind the mountains of the upper Surselva, casting long shadows down the valley. The Canadian drives along the dirt road, sending dust flying everywhere, then vanishes around the bend. The farmhand's sitting behind the hut on a log.

It's a clear, starry night. The dairyman's lying outside the pigpen in the grass. The bottle's lying at his side. Fazandin's digging a ditch around the dairyman. He sticks his spade into the ground, leans on the shoulder with his boot, lifts some earth out, sticks the spade back in, and lifts some more out, continuing like that till he's dug all the way around. Keep on digging, Fazandin, keep on digging, deeper and deeper around the snoring dairyman.

Two shadows are under the boiler. The man's holding his hand up to his eyes, against the light of the torch. He turns on his side and covers the woman up to her neck with the blanket. When the cows are in the cowshed, the milking machines are pumping, the fire in the big stove is blazing, morning has broken and the sun's slowly brightening the sky, bathing the peak of Tumpiv in yellow and forcing its shadow down the mountain, the two shadows under the boiler with a display have disappeared.

Alig drives his Rapid and its trailer around the corner of the hut. He drives across the yard and onto the hay meadow behind the hay barn, where the grass is knee-high. In the hay meadow, he separates the trailer and the Rapid and prepares the blades. He ties the rope around the crank, pulls it, *capiergna*, ties the rope around the crank again, and adjusts a lever. He pulls the rope and the engine breaks the morning silence.

Alig's in the hay meadow, mowing. To and fro he goes in the meadow with his Rapid, his sleeves rolled up and in his old army boots, segs on the soles. The Rapid's rattling evenly. Like a great general, Alig steers his machine across the meadow, mowing down hundreds at once. Now and again he stops, takes a gulp from the big half-empty bottle of Calanda under the cut hay, that's good, that is, then keeps going till he's mown them all down and the second bottle's also empty, and he reattaches the trailer and, *tgauadia*, vanishes around the bend on the dirt road.

With his Justy, the dairyman takes bale of hay after bale of hay from the hay meadow to the hay barn, on the roof of the Justy. The dogs trot along behind him. The swineherd stands with his hayfork in the hayloft and arranges the hay in the corners. The goat's next to the hayloft. It snatches the fresh hay. The dogs run after the Justy, over to where the next load's being tied up in a cloth. The dairyman stays where he is.

Late afternoon arrives, the hay's in the hayloft and the two herders come up the hill from the hut with the dogs, past the cairn, and vanish behind the next set of hills, along the fence, up in the direction of Sez Ner.

The farmhand's at the pigpen with his hands in his pockets. Standing there in his boots, he looks across to the other side of the valley, where the village is embedded at the foot of Tumpiv. He sees, in the meadows at the end of the village, how the workers on this clear summer Monday are using machinery to dig the ground for the golf course and level the meadows.

The one with the limp won't eat. She's chained up in the cowshed until the herd and the cowherd and his hat and the dogs have gone. The farmhand unchains her, the shed door stays shut though. The farmhand brings her down some hay, throws it in the feeding trough. The one with the limp sniffs at the hay but doesn't touch it. She lies down. Water, she doesn't want either. The farmhand leaves the water where it is, beside the one with the limp, runs his hand along her back and leaves the cowshed.

The tourists drive up on the dirt road and stop when they get to the cowherd with the alpenroses he's picked in his hand. The tourists keep the engine running, want to buy the bouquet from the cowherd. The cowherd's gaze wanders across the slopes covered in alpenroses by the side of the track, and back to the tourists in the car with their hats and sunglasses.

Go up for the eggs, the dairyman tells the swineherd, who is standing in the pigsty with the hose. The swineherd climbs the ladder to the coop, above the pigsty. He pushes aside the hens that are sitting on their eggs and puts the eggs in his cap. Three lousy eggs, the dairyman says, he didn't drag hens all the way up here for them just to eat and fuckin fuck all day. He takes the eggs from his cap and returns to the hut through the pigsty. Including those 3, that's 131 eggs this summer so far. 14 of which broke: 3 fell out of the coop, 11 broke on the way from the coop to the hut, 2 of which broke in the swineherd's trouser pocket. Not included are the eggs laid outside the coop, so still lying around somewhere.

The cowherd's perched on a stone in the fog by the boggy meadow, and whittling his stick. He can hear the cowbells but, in this soup, can't see the tail of a single cow. Beside the cowherd sits the old gray dog. The dope's not with him, he didn't want that one along today anyway. The old gray dog sits, impatient, beside him, whimpering now and again and pushing his nose up into the cowherd's armpit, making the cowherd push him away. The old gray dog raises its head again and pricks its ears. The cowherd doesn't stroke the old dog, he doesn't scratch its chest, doesn't tickle the back of its head. You'll lose your bite otherwise and not follow me any more eh, the cowherd says to the gray dog, I *will* stroke you if you can get the herd back out of this fuckin fog.

The cowherd's boot is sinking into the bog. The boot's filling with water. The cowherd pulls his leg out and the boot stays where it is. He stands on one leg, still wearing the dripping sock, and pulls the boot back out. The cowherd empties the water from the boot. What would it be like to sink into the bog. Up to your knees. Up to your hips. Up to your neck, and then completely.

The cowherd's crossing the meadow with the stick in his hand. The gray dog's running ahead of him. The wet sock inside his boot makes every step sound as if it was wet snow he was walking through.

The cow belonging to Giosch has a slight squint.

The ram with the plaster casts is lying next to the farmhand behind the cowshed, on the planks over the slurry pit. The farmhand's reading his book. From time immemorial, the Romansh have often moved abroad. Some for pleasure, others out of necessity. There wasn't enough to go around everyone at home. And only some of them could have an existence under another roof in their home village or elsewhere in the small region they were born in. The farmhand stubs out his Select, lets it fall through the cracks into the slurry.

The leaflets from tourist information are hanging on the wall of the hut and in the parlor. Sez Ner is the center of Surselva. A modest height, it has everything that makes a mountain a mountain. The steep slopes, the shadows, the ridges, the peak, the cairn, the cross. At the back of the mountain, the rock face to crash to your death from. Unassuming, it stands there, putting up with whatever goes on round about, braving the weather in all its forms, surrounded by mighty comrades with awe-inspiring names, all of them closer to the sky. On the front of the tourist information leaflets is a picture of the dairyman, on high gloss paper, standing at the pigpen with one hand leaning on his Justy 4x4. The other hand's on his hip and he has crossed his legs. In the background, three pigs' snouts and a jackdaw on the fencepost, before the mountain backdrop and the bright blue sky. Above the image in huge letters: A Unique Experience of Nature on the Alp.

The farmhand is putting milking grease on his eyebrows.

The cheese cellar's filling up. The longer the summer goes on and the more cheese is in the cellar, the fatter the dairyman gets. The two herders sit behind the cowshed in the twilight, worrying the dairyman has put weight on. The cowherd says, if this continues, we'll have to adapt the dairyman's Justy. He hands the swineherd the cigar he swapped with the farmers for butter from the alp. The best thing would be to remove the front seat so the dairyman could drive the Justy from the back. The swineherd nods and draws on the Rössli.

The herdsmen on the alp wear clothes you'd hardly notice. It's not some show we're putting on, the dairyman says. The animals are startled when the herdsmen on the alp turn up looking as if they're going to a children's party.

The cowherd from Alp Prada is coming along the dirt road with his dog. His unsteady step is recognizable, even from afar. He's wearing a bright woolen cap and carrying a black umbrella. It's a longhaired dog, its legs too short for working on the alp. A stick, the cowherd doesn't have. He has the umbrella instead. That, he drags onto the meadow with him. That, he takes into the hut with him. What is it he wants, the dairyman asks. Have you any rennet, the cowherd says, his hand reaching for his dirty woolen cap, the boss sent me. The dairyman shakes his head. It's not a lot he needs, the cowherd says, two days' worth. The dairyman shakes his head. Not even the last of some. No.

Old Pieder tells them on Sunday his uncle emigrated to America in the Thirties. His hat's in his hand, his bald head shining in the sun. Thirty-six-and-a-half years later, he returned in the middle of the winter. An act of God didn't help then either, the next summer he vanished again, au revoir, forever. Seems he died the same day his cow was born.

The dairyman comes out of the hay barn and across the yard with the big axe. Behind him, the cowherd, rolling a log he stands in the yard beside the fountain, where the chickens peck the grain in the dirt and the scraps from breakfast. At the first attempt, the cowherd grabs the chicken selected by the dairyman and holds its legs tight. Hold its legs tight and swing it around, the dairyman says, faster. Come here, give the useless thing to me. The dairyman spins the chicken around until the black chicken has its beak open and its head hangs forward. *Vualà*, he says to the cowherd who holds the sharpened axe out to him and takes a step back, *fertic lustic*. The dairyman puts the chicken with the outstretched neck down on the log, the other chickens have long since withdrawn to behind the cowshed, holds the axe with his outstretched arm over the chicken's throat, doesn't move at all for a moment, closes his left eye as if taking aim, swings the axe with his outstretched arm back as far as his head. The cowherd takes another step back. The blade of the axe flashes in the sun, a gulp from the creatures of the alp, the dairyman grimaces. Chop.

The swineherd's painting the cows' horns. He goes through the cowshed with the paint pot and brush. There are dribbles of paint all the way through. He paints the cows' right horns. The cows at the bottom of the cowshed get a yellow horn. The cows in the middle of the cowshed get a blue horn, and the cows at the top of the cowshed a red one. Order must be.

The cows got into the pasture below the alp, Alig says, his pasture, his spring pasture, and ate half of what was there. He waves his walking stick, and you'll rue the day, he says with his one leg shorter than the other, pointing the tip of his stick at the pale-as-cheese belly of the dairyman, who is lying in the sun on a blanket outside the pigpen. The dairyman gets up and puts his hands on his hips. Alig is a bucket-length taller than him.

The vet puts the green apron on. He pulls his plastic gloves on and tells the farmhand to get the lame bride up on her feet. The farmhand taps her rump with the toe of his boot, hits her back with the palm of his hand. The sound echoes between the shed and the hut. The one with the limp stays where she is. The farmhand grabs her tail and bends it as though about to tie a knot while, with his thumb and forefinger, the swineherd grabs the cow by the nose. Her dry nose.

The bull's behind the cowshed at the entrance to the hay barn from the hay meadow. The swineherd needs to get into the hay barn. The sacks of pig feed are there. He climbs onto the wooden fence. When he jumps down on the other side, the bull turns to him. When the swineherd starts to run, the bull starts to run.

Any time the dairyman comes to the pasture, the old gray dog runs over to him. The dairyman takes up position on a hillock and whistles to the dog to run along the bottom, to run along the left, till he has all the cows where he wants them. A cowherd without a dog is only half a cowherd, the cowherd thinks to himself. Did you see that, the dairyman says to the cowherd, without a dog you're worth about as much as a swineherd. He strokes the dog's snout, turns away and goes. The cowherd holds the dog tightly by the collar.

The swineherd's behind the closed door of the hay barn with two bucketfuls of pig feed and a bull at the door of the barn. The sun shines through the cracks in the barn door.

The dope's sniffing at the black feathers down from the yard while the cows are in the cowshed with full udders in the late afternoon, licking the last of yesterday's salt from the trough.

Inside the hut, the dairyman brings macaroni with grated cheese into the parlor. The farmhand's sitting with his book, beneath the cow bell with the heavy clapper. You'll end up in a cassock if you read too much of that *ora-pro-nobis* stuff, the dairyman says. The cowherd comes down the stairs with the new Chianti for the dairyman. But with your eight fingers, they wouldn't give you a damn biretta anyhow, the dairyman says and leaves the parlor. The swineherd comes down the stairs, hangs his cap on the antlers beside the door, and gets the bread from the cupboard. The dairyman brings the boiled chicken into the parlor and puts it down in the middle of the table, *vualà*.

Gieri breaks his leg, nearly. He's lying on his stomach in the washing cellar with his leg down the drain. Because the water's not draining away properly, the farmhand has removed the grate in the cellar to scoop the water out with the bucket. Gieri always has his nose in the air, doesn't see the ground beneath his feet.

The dairyman's in the cool cheese cellar, counting the wheels of cheese. The farmhand stands behind him, takes the boards with the cheese from the surround and rubs the cheese with salt and whey. The dairyman watches with his hands on his hips and a bazooka in his mouth. You still have to take the wheels of cheese in the salt bath out too, he says. The farmhand doesn't answer. The dairyman goes out. He comes back in at intervals.

Fazandin is coming out of the forest. His spade, he's carrying on his shoulder. He walks along the perimeter fence, up towards Sez Ner. He has a hat, covered in dust, on his head. His gray eyes look out from under the hat and he rubs his nose. In between times he stops, kneels down on the meadow, crawls around on the meadow, plucks grass from the meadow, looks up again, rubs his nose, takes the spade beside him in the grass, stands up and continues his climb. Fazandin, Fazandin, *ti nas fin*, you fine nose, you, he sings, tearing out more grass and continuing to climb, with his spade on his shoulder. His silhouette pales in the thick fog, then vanishes completely.

The one with the limp doesn't want to get up. Does nothing but lie outside the shed. She's lost weight, you can see her ribs through the hide. The vet says there's nothing more he can do. His son carts his case along behind him, past the dairyman to the 4x4. The 4x4 follows the Justy along the dirt road and through the fog.

The wind sweeps across the alp. Across the valley, in the dark night, one alpine fire after another lines up on the curve of the mountain, above the treeline. Between them, one fire that is many times bigger than the others. That's Alp Rueun, the dairyman says, looking through his binoculars again. The flames climb into the air, lash out in the wind, the hut's on fire. In the forest below the hut on Alp Rueun, lights are climbing up the mountain. By the time the first lights reach the treeline, the flames on Alp Rueun have tired themselves out.

The nail on his big toe is hurting. The swineherd put the wrong boots on and a cow stood on it. It feels like the toe is stuck in a screw clamp. The nail's turning purple. The swineherd bores the point of his Swiss army knife through the purple nail. He presses the liquid under the nail out through the hole he's made with the knife. The pressure eases. A few nights later, the nail parts company with the toe.

Georg, the cowbell now over his shoulder, loads his gun and takes up position before the one with the limp. He strokes her between the horns, presses the muzzle against her brow and bang. The one with the limp slumps to the ground. The swineherd's behind the fence. He has a tinny taste in his mouth.

With their high-gloss leaflets in their hands, the day-trippers are standing around the cheese kettle, beside the tourist guide from tourist information, who is holding a red flag with a white cross. The dairyman, with a dripping skimmer in his right hand, welcomes them and explains things. The cameras flash and the guide nods as if he knows all this already and a lot more besides. The flock of guests, bunched close together, marvel at the demonstration, not realizing that outside, beneath the steamed-up windows, their rucksacks are being ransacked by the herders.

The bull roars and climbs on. The cow moves to the side, the bull slips off and has to re-insert his dripping carrot. As soon as the bull gets anywhere close, the cow shifts away. The cow is now tied to the fence behind the hut. The bull climbs on again, throws its forelegs along the cow's back, like fence posts. The cow's back gives, as though her bones were about to collapse under the weight. The bull is now thrusting, short, strong thrusts, he sticks out his tongue and his eyes are rolling.

To say thank you for the cheese, Köbi sticks his hand out to the dairyman and his tongue out at the dog. The dope jumps up and bites Köbi's finger. His Rössli falls to the ground. Köbi lets out a yelp and drops the cheese. He kicks out at the dog with his boot. Köbi picks a stone up, *huara cleppers*, and hits the burned-out bucket lying among the scraps behind the fountain for the chickens.

Boys, the dairyman roars. The herders are lying up on the roof of the hut. It's not what you'd call comfortable. The little plastic hooks dig into your back. The roof of the hut is a good place. The dairyman doesn't think to look for them there. And they can remove the plastic hooks. That doesn't take any wizardry.

Clemens—who likes the sound of his own voice—has fallen in love, it seems. Never out of the pub, he is, and he can't keep his eyes off the landlord's wife's calves. I warned him, you'll get a sore stomach, staring like that, Gieri says. He'd only ever a sore stomach once, Clemens. Years ago, seemingly. Seven snails he took for it that time, still alive they were, he washed them down with three Hail Marys. Never had any trouble since.

Just down from the hut before the mountain backdrop, the bull's lying in the grass. You two bring the bull back up to Alp Prada, the dairyman says to the herders. The bull runs along the road that gradually rounds the curve of the mountain. At Alp Prada, the road ends. From there, there isn't a proper road anymore, around the mountain to Alp Naul. From Alp Naul, a new road continues around the curve of the mountain, the valley ever narrowing now, to Alp Nova. At Alp Nova, the valley is at its narrowest, and at the top, Val Lumnezia begins to open.

The farmhand's lying at the edge of the forest in Stavonas Sut, in the damp moss beneath a red fir, with his book in his hand and drawing on his cigar. The flies buzz around his head in the windless summer's afternoon. In the book he reads: The call for reduced working hours has been making itself heard for years. Nearly half of the workers no longer work on Saturdays. What do these people do in their free time? A farmer: they sit in the restaurant all day Saturday, when the farmer is still supposed to work, and all day Sunday. They talk politics while drinking alcohol and set a bad example for farmers. Those who are still farmers are good people. Laborers and employees are a bunch of troublemakers.

Around the corner of the hut comes a man with big hands. He asks for the dairyman. He's just gone off, and his farmhand, he's not here. The man waits, walks over to the pigpen before the mountain backdrop, comes back after a while. When will the dairyman be back, he's taking a while, can I try the cheese while I wait, no, the swineherd says. He's the dairyman's uncle, you see, the man with the big hands says, and he'd like to try the cheese. The swineherd shakes his head. Could he have a coffee, at least. The swineherd says he's not allowed to let anyone into the hut. The man gets up from the wooden bench with the engraved plaque outside the hut. He really has to go now, had come over Sez Ner especially to try the cheese. The swineherd sticks to his guns.

The village policeman's at the door, asking to see the dairyman. The farmhand says he's not here. The dairyman, as is well known, broke the finger of a tourist, a highly respected politician from the lowlands, incidentally, with the skimmer. He needs to take a statement. The village policeman goes over to the pigpen. He takes his hat off, looks across at the mountain panorama and nods. Seeing as he's here already, and if he has to wait anyhow, could he have a glass of milk and a piece of cheese, he asks the farmhand.

On every wheel of cheese is a plastic logo. Under the plastic logo is the date.

The visitors come at dusk while the milking's being done and shoulder crates of beer into the warm parlor. They've cigarettes in the corner of their mouths and cigars behind their ears, bottles of schnapps in their hands, snuff boxes in their trouser pockets, they've their sleeves rolled up, revealing lower arms like logs, hang their hats on the antlers, sit down at the parlor table like they're in no hurry to get back up again, loosen their belts to sit comfortably and, in keeping with the old custom, start with a schnapps. They strike matches on their raw hands and light fat cigars and the first of them are already drunk and merry, the parlor heated and full of smoke, when the evening milking is done and the dairyman and his farmhand leave the milking machines where they are, next to the cows, can untie their milking stools and join the others. As thirsty as camels, they are, as if they'd run here from Rome without a single break, simultaneously they take two bottles from the crates, open them with their teeth, spit the tops across the floor, raise the bottles, one, two, three, *hauruc*, and having toasted each other, bang the table with the bottom of the bottles and start to drink.

The visitors have slipped off, with the exception of one, when the two herders, at daybreak, during the milking, tidy up the beer bottles on the table and on the floor, and remove the tins, full to the brim with butts, wipe away the tobacco crumbs and ash beneath the table and the bench, and collect the bottle tops, scattered across the entire floor like coins. The last of the guests is still at the table. He's peed his trousers and is snoring.

The inspectors are down in the cheese cellar, their papers clipped onto the clipboards in their hands. Their pens move across the columns, circling and crossing things. They flick through the papers attached to the folders. The inspectors cut into the cheese. They cut cigarette-shaped pieces out. They push the cigarette butts back into the cheese so no one can tell which cheese they cut into. Beneath the window, in the bedroom, are the wheels of cheese that rolled across the ground that morning. The dairyman's outside the cheese cellar and, for a good half hour, walks impatiently, to and fro and with his eyebrows furled, as if he was about to make his Easter confession. With dry handshakes, the inspectors leave the hut. You'll be hearing from us.

Between the hills, at the perimeter fence below Sez Ner, in the alpenroses, lies the still-born calf. The dope bites and tugs at the calf's ear. His paws get a grip on its head, and he digs his claws into the brute's scalp. He tugs at the ear, lets it go. He circles the lifeless beast, gets hold of the ear with his canines, sinks his teeth in, growls, then his molars get in on the act. He growls, pulls the ear of the calf back, finally tears it off, and eats it.

Coffee, nothing but coffee. Coffee was the best thing to drink, out in the field. Coffee was the best for thirst. The thing to do when it was hot was have a hot drink. Other drinks just made you more thirsty, his grandmother always said.

In the parlor, on the left, across from the antlers, is the drawer without a handle. It's the second from the bottom, the one with the sweets in it. The herders intercept the sweets before they get to the drawer. The dairyman keeps a close eye on the drawer, almost as much as on the cheese cellar. The farmers are gradually realizing that the way to get butter from the alp is via the herders. Behind the hut, next to the pile of wood in the corner, beneath the roof-wing that reaches way down—there, in the beams, they hide what they swap.

The cowherd lifts the dead calf and slips the carcass into the plastic bag. He ties the bag with a double knot. With the plastic bag on his shoulder, the cowherd walks down the ridge-trail. His silhouette is dark in the evening light. The sun casts long shadows along the valley. The peaks of the mountains are coated with honey.

In the village, Lucas has been run over. And I'm glad he has, Georg says. Giachen ran him over, after midnight, driving home from the bar. In the middle of the road Lucas was, it seems, after the big bend into the little bend next to the church. He'd had nothing but hassle with the stubborn ass anyhow.

The ladder's leaning against the roof of the barn. Two rungs are missing. The farmhand is up on the roof, mending the hole in the roof so there are no more leaks into the hayloft. When the afternoon arrives, the hole in the roof is no more. The farmhand stands on the gable, looking across the valley. There's not a cloud in the sky. Shoulder to shoulder, peak after peak rises, marking a border, as if—on the other side of this great border—there was nothing else.

When the dope turns up outside the hut suddenly, after the milking, the dairyman unties his milking stool. When the dairyman approaches him, the dog moves away, whimpering. The dairyman follows him. At the pigpen, he finally gets his mits on him.

The teacher points to the swineherd. Him there, who knows what you call that one. One of the girls says, that's the dairyman, no, the cowherd, no, the mucker-outer for the stables, correct, the teacher says, write that down everyone. The pupils write in their blue jotters. What does a mucker-outer do, mucks out the stables, another girl answers. Ursula, the teacher says, what have I told you about speaking before putting your hand up, sorry, sir, the girl says, correct, I'll ask you again, what does a muckerouter do. The pupils' hands shoot up. A boy at the back gets to answer. He mucks out the stables, correct.

Teachers, I don't trust, the dairyman says, with a serious look in his eyes. Teachers are the kings of their own kingdoms. Dangerous, that is. They point their thumbs up or down, like Pontius fuckin Pilate. I'm done with teachers, says the dairyman. He'd had one teacher, same damn idiot for nine years, a white overall he wore, and he took a stick to the children like they were cows. Nearly took the ear off of him, he did. He's never trusted ones in white overalls and black suits since.

On the First of August, the cowherd and the swineherd are up on the alp at the foot of Sez Ner with the herd in driving snow. Can you do my flies up again, the cowherd asks the swineherd, he can't manage himself, he says, rubbing his frozen hands against a cow while the wind blasts snow at the creatures on the alp in the morning on their national day.

The dairyman, in his white apron, is sitting beneath the crucifix in the parlor. Christ's hanging on the crucifix. His right hand's missing. The village policeman is opposite the dairyman, on the stool behind the typewriter. Name, date of birth, place of residence, marital status. The village policeman slowly presses key after key on his Hermes. As dusk begins to fall, he whips the sheet of paper out of the typewriter and puts it in his briefcase. The village policeman puts his hat on what little hair he has still and thanks the dairyman for the milk, the butter from the alp, the yoghurt from the alp, the two wheels of cheese from the alp, plus the Schabziger and the soft cheese — and leaves their hut on the alp, whistling.

It's been raining for four days. The herd makes its way along the dirt road, won't be climbing anywhere today. The first of the cows round the bend at the final gully before the border of the alp, leading the pack is Old Dear, owned by Toni Liung, in her lee others from the same stable, and the rest of the straggling field. The first of the cows reach the pasture at the border of the alp, cross it where the pastures below the alp meet the alp itself. On down from their own pasture, on the slopes of his spring pasture, is Luis with his scythe. He raises his hand.

The black ram with the white patch on its head has put on weight. You can hardly feel its ribs now, the farmhand says, taking a sip of his coffee. The ram has put on weight since its plaster casts were removed. The makings of a good feast, says the dairyman in his white apron, without looking up. He's flicking through the *Blick* the farmers left lying around, a week past on Sunday. The ram's mine at the end of the summer, the farmhand says. He can have the goat, he tells the dairyman, and the chickens and all, for all he cares, but not the ram. The dairyman finishes flicking through the paper, folds it, gets up and puts it back on the windowsill, beside the radio with the bent aerial. To hell with the fuckin goat.

Luis with the scar over his eye is on the bench outside the cowshed, carving a plug. Well, well. The swineherd draws on his Rössli. His great-grandmother made it to one hundred and three, he says, hadn't been able to walk anymore, stand anymore, couldn't see anything in the end, hear anything, hadn't been able to speak anymore either. He'd had the greatest respect for his great-grandmother. Luis continues to carve his plug, *vualà*, he says, putting the plug aside, the knife and all, to treat himself to a new Rössli, fresh from the box.

What's new down in the village, Luis asks back. *Nuot*, nothing, absolutely nothing, and to make matters worse, things are all the same still. Wait a minute, Luis says and goes into the cowshed. He hands the cowherd a full glass. There's a bit of truth in there, he says, and his gray stubble smiles. Down in the village, the woman next door, chop, had cut the heads of his wife's sunflowers off, he says. His great-grandmother had always said the valley was narrow and the oldest woman in the valley was jealousy. He relights his Rössli as it's gone out. His grandfather, though, said there was only one cure for jealousy and that was chopping wood. The only cure for jealousy was chopping wood.

The farmers are sitting with their hats at the parlor table, drawing on their cigars and drinking coffee with schnapps, play the card, not this one, play the other one, the trump, play the trump I tell you, no not that card, play the other one, you've still got the other one, why are you playing this one when you've still got that one, you must still have the trump, they're not all out yet, what have you still got, if not the trump.

Gallopper, Gallopper is the best beer of all, the dairyman says. Try Gallopper once, and you'll never try anything else. I don't dislike Calanda either. Soon be all the same anyhow, eh.

Lightning killed three of her-across-the-way's cattle, the farmer says at the cowshed door, beneath the crucifix with the fir twig. The porch is dripping. Friday, three of them, she herself was lucky. He puts out his hand to feel the rain. The other hand's in his trouser pocket. The ways of the Lord are mysterious. The rain beats down on the yard, heavier and heavier. He himself was lucky too, none of his bit the dust. If it keeps going like this though, sooner or later it's everyone's turn, eh. The wind buffets the shed and hut, whips the rain against the wall of the shed, the shutters against the wall of the hut.

The swineherd is carrying a wooden door across the yard. The door's on his back and he's holding the sides tight above his head. The wooden door forces his head forward. The shadow of the swineherd stretches across the yard.

The cows are in the pasture in the rain, the pasture that soon won't have a blade of grass, below the fog boundary. Sez Ner can't be seen. The church bells can be heard ringing from the village below. Luis is on the peening bench, sharpening his scythe, with a Rössli hanging from his mouth. Religion is what's hanging between your legs, he says, wiping his brow with his sleeve. His wife goes to church every Sunday, he himself only reluctantly, not because I don't believe, he does believe actually, just don't expect him to get up early and go to church to repeat whatever drivel the cleric spouts, parrot-like. He takes a gulp from his cup. He speaks to God when he mows the meadow by hand, that's the best way to speak to him.

The dairyman's lying beside the pigs with a headache and a scratched face. The bull from the Alp Prada got him up on its horns when he tried to chase it. The bull lifted the dairyman and hurled him away, ripped his trousers front and back. The dairyman managed to escape under the fence before the bull could charge again. Some pigs that have escaped sniff at the trousers of the sleeping dairyman.

Luis scrapes the broom from the cowshed across the stones outside. Why not stay up here, isn't it nice in the mountains in summer, he says. The young ones would rather run a mile, down the valley, down to the lowlands and across the lowlands, and even further down, as far as the sea and across the sea, yes, to America if it worked out, and never come back. Oh well, he pauses, he did understand somehow, somehow he did understand, the val-

ley and resentment were inseparable, they were. Like the door of
the hut and the resin on it.

The milking machines tick like alarm clocks. They tick as if there
was a time-fuse inside them. They tick and, any minute, everything will explode with a terrible bang you'll be able to hear in
the whole valley, a deadly explosion rising dozens of meters into
the air and leaving a crater you wouldn't have thought possible.
The cowherd hears the tick of the milking machines even when
he's finished milking. They tick in his head till it's time to milk
again. His heartbeat is in sync with the milking machines.

The farmhand is blowing up the washing-up glove. The orange
glove starts to swell and to raise finger after finger. The inflated
washing-up glove resembles a swollen hand. The glove can be
slipped on, but only with difficulty. Without the gloves, the water's too hot and the powder eats into your skin and ruins your
hands.

The cows eat three times as much when snow's on its way, the
farmer says. Plus, they get restless. You'd think they weren't going to see any more food before the spring, way they demolish
the last blades of grass. If the cows smell snow on its way, they
don't sleep. If the cows smell snow on its way, they stop being
so fussy, and devour whatever grass there still is, just, before the
alp's snowed in.

The swineherd's sitting on a pig. The pig squeals and runs around
in circles till it stops, still unable to explain the sudden weight on
its back. Tiredness must be to blame for the pig's hoofs sinking
especially deep into the muck today.

Clemens's cow is in heat. She's in the bedroom of the two herders where the window's open and, across the valley, Tumpiv can be seen with its cloud-hat. To the right of Tumpiv is Kistenstock, a mountain that looks as if God sawed the top half off. Kistenstock which, instead of a peak, now has a surface the size of a lower pasture.

The swineherd can hear the dairyman shouting even louder, *huara tgaulom*, the dirt on the ceiling's dropping into the cheese kettle, is this 'cause things are going too well for him, or what. The swineherd grabs the cow by the strap on the bell and gets his thumb and forefinger in its nose. Squeezing, he forces the head of the cow away from the window. Forcing the head down, he pulls the cow around, pulls her with him, out into the hall, past the boiler with the display, and out of the hut. He can hear the dairyman stomping up the stairs.

The clouds are gradually dispersing. The days of rain have made the ground softer. The cowherd from the next alp is outside her hut, wringing the wet sheet out. She wrings so hard, the tendons stick out in her bare arms and her bare arms start to tremble. She wrings as if it was a ram she was trying to strangle, always letting go at the last minute and starting all over again, till the sheet is crinkled and she hangs it up on the clothesline stretching from the corner of the hut to the fountain. Her dog lies beside her with its head on its paws and looks at the sheet. The sheet flutters in the morning wind.

The old gray dog trots along behind the cowherd, the cowherd's stick between its teeth.

There was a fire in the village a few days ago, the milk inspector says as they eat before milking. Oh, did they not see anything. As soon as a few clouds come along up here, you can't see the tail on the nearest cow, the dairyman says. Mm, mm. Well, Thursday night it was, or Wednesday night. Wednesday night or Thursday night, oh, he wasn't sure anymore, or maybe it was Thursday night, yes, yes, Thursday, he remembered now, he'd been at choir practice before it happened, yes, yes, so Thursday night it was, or a week ago on Thursday.

The house of this—this lowlander went on fire. Boy had bought it in the winter, an old shack. They'd all been amazed, what was he thinking, with that. The dairyman pours some schnapps into his coffee. Burned down to the ground. The village fire brigade did a good job, or half the village would've burned down too. Boy had gone to Majorca, on holiday with his wife, two days before, away, the bastard was, in Majorca, and *voilà*. Good thing the village fire brigade was so brave, says the milk inspector. You wouldn't want a repeat of that disaster, back in '24, when seven houses, seven large stables, and seven small stables burned down. The fire truck, a Magirus, had to come up from Chur, to calm the raging flames that time.

The pig's squealing and gasping. Its nose ring was inserted too far back in its nose. The pig's breathing heavily and with difficulty and blood's dripping from its nose. We'll not get that back out again. The pig's lying against the wall, its open mouth in the dirt, breathing heavily, no longer squealing. Some of the other pigs sniff around at it, press their snouts against its stomach, move their docked tails to and fro. Above the pigsty, the hens sit on their eggs, looking down at the pigs.

The mountain stream bubbles over the stones, down the middle of the meadow. A beetle is on its back in the water, at the side of the stream. Its legs are moving but it can't get back out. The stream sweeps the beetle away, down into the valley. The stream grows in size, the closer it gets to the valley floor, and changes its face. The longer it gets, the more dangerous it makes its banks. Ever since the stream swept his uncle down its rock face, the swineherd's been afraid in the dark. In the dark, his uncle is there, among the dead.

Fazandin's down on all fours among the cows in the pasture. He's tearing out grass and warbling to himself: white mustard, white mustard, mushed mustard attacks stubborn phlegm, clears the head and eases toothache. On all fours, he goes back to his spade in the grass. He smells the herbs around the stones, takes his spade and climbs the slope with it. He turns up again, in the hills, before reaching the boundary of the fog and really disappearing.

The wing mirror of the Subaru is broken. The mirror's hanging off, on three wires. A farmer from Alp Prada hit it, with his red tractor. His Aebi. The farmhand saw him. The dairyman doesn't know who it was that ripped his mirror off. Giachen says, you don't need wing mirrors, and definitely not a rear mirror. Seems he never reverses. Only ever goes forward. If ever he gets lost, which happens once in every three blue moons, he just keeps going, seemingly. There's always a road that'll take you back, he claims, even if you keep going forward.

The pigs are lying in the mud behind the sty. They don't move. Are lying there like sacks of potatoes. From time to time, an ear moves. From time to time, a pig grunts. Then all is quiet again.

The goat's standing on the edge of the fountain, the tourists are taking photographs. The goat takes a drink, the tourists take a photo. The goat shows its horns, the tourists take a photo. The goat nibbles at the bouquet of flowers above the water tap, the tourists take a photo. The goat nibbles at the fresh bread, the tourists take a photo. The goat jumps down from the fountain, the tourists take a photo.

The roar of engines breaks the silence of the alp. Right at the front is Alig with his Rapid and a huge load of wood. Behind Alig is Toni Liung with his Aebi. Köbi's beside him in the passenger seat. Toni Liung and Köbi both have orange earmuffs on their ears. The dogs leap along the dirt road to bark at the engines. The dogs give way, jump onto the upper slope and bark at the engines from the side. They run alongside the vehicles, across the hills with the withering alpenroses. The farmers sitting in the vehicles aren't impressed.

The dairyman's sitting at the table in the hut, beneath the crucifix with the dried fir twig, with a glass of strong schnapps and is turning the dial of the radio with the bent aerial when the three farmers enter the parlor with smoking mouths and firewater they distilled themselves. They keep their hats on, don't take the hats off, as if about to draw their guns any minute.

They're a total mess, that crowd at Alp Prada, the dairyman says. He's standing up, one hand leaning on the pile of wood. Once at six and once at eight, they milk, I wouldn't be sending my cows up there if I was the farmer. The two farmers behind the hut with earmuffs on their ears nod. And if the cowshed's in that kind of state, I don't want to know what their cheese cellar looks like. The dairyman folds his arms, the farmers nod. Lazy sods, they are, having themselves a nice summer and no more than that, don't you two try to tell me for one minute either that fuckin crowd can cope. No one actually knows how many people are on that alp, he shakes his head, that's no way to manage an alp, and that's that.

Looks like we're in for one hell of a storm this evening, says Alig, who has one leg shorter than the other, better close the windows. *Tgauadia*, says the dairyman when, in the late afternoon, the farmers are sitting on their vehicles, Toni Liung and Köbi right at the front. Alig, behind them, looks back again. He hasn't forgiven the herdsmen for letting the cows get into his spring pasture. The dust whirls up on the road. The flies buzz around the head of the dairyman, who is outside the hut with his hands in his pockets, watching the gunslingers go.

Melancholy dries out your bones, it says in the book. Don't throw your old shoes away before you have new ones. Buy truth but don't sell it. Better to carry your cross than to drag it along behind you. The farmhand flicks, flicks, flicks through the book. At the back of the book, pictures of: Pope John XXIII, John F. Kennedy, Pope Paul VI, the bishop, with the kind permission of the fatherland. *Autoritads ecclesiasticus*: (from top to bottom) Pope Paul VI, bishop of Chur, vicar generals. The chapter of the cathedral: dean of the cathedral, deacon of the cathedral, cathedral scolasticus, cathedral cantor (vacant), cathedral custos. The farmhand strokes the ears of the black ram with the white patch.

What do I need to do, asks the dairyman, but all done and dusted otherwise, eh, we're not exactly savages up here, right. All that stuff about the dairyman singing and his songs, tra-la-la etcetera, you only find that in books. That's the kind of stuff dreamt up by tourism experts and pencil-sharpener types as they sit around in cafes all day. *Huara politica da caffe*.

The cowherd has a toothache. A tooth at the back on the right is sore. Dr Tomaschett, in a black suit, puts his leather case down on the table in the hut. Let me see your poverty, he says, adjusting his glasses on his nose. Aha, opens his case and takes out the forceps. Not known anyone to die of that yet, just so you know, but first drink this, he says, handing the cowherd the glass before plunging the forceps into the cowherd's mouth. The swineherd's amazed at the brute force of the old gentleman.

It's a clear morning. Last night's storm is almost forgotten. It thundered until deep in the night, lightning struck all around the alp and set a fir on fire at the edge of the forest, down from the hut. A few scraps of cloud in the sky still. From Sez Ner, the cowherd can see the burned-out hut on Alig's spring pasture. It's still smoking. Jackdaws wait quietly on the fence posts of the perimeter fence with the neighboring alp.

The two herders are behind the hut, behind the mountain of wood, chopping wood beneath the bright blue sky. Sweat is running down their chins and necks. The swineherd slams the wooden mallet on the log, whack, that's for the dairyman, he says, panting, he lifts the mallet back behind his head, whack, for every single one of those bastards, says the cowherd, whack, for the dairyman, whack, whack, for the rat-catchers, whack, for the dairyman, whack-whack for the wood gods, whack, *per la patria*, whack.

In the evening, the swineherd's sitting behind the cowshed in the wheelbarrow. The wheelbarrow has an arm missing. The swineherd has a Rössli in his mouth. He looks across at Tumpiv, its peak still glowing in the evening sun, and blows smoke rings into the mild alpine evening.

The roar of engines chokes to a stop. The light in the cowshed goes out slowly. The cowherd steps out of the lean-to behind the cowshed onto the concrete slab, and slams the engine room door shut. The last weak sunrays fall across the valley. He takes

his fork from the pocket of his blue overall and scratches a mark
in the wall.

Giosch's cow knocks the milking machine over with its leg. *Sma-
ledida portga*, the dairyman roars, booting the cow in the stomach and making it wince. Fleabag of a farmer, that Giosch. He
tries to turn the machine on again. The cow kicks out as soon as
the machine pulls on its teats. The dairyman, with the milking
stool around his waist, hits out at the cow's shin. Get me the milk
pail. The dairyman bends under the cow and milks her by hand.
Slaughter them, these two fuckin fleabags of Giosch's, slaughter
them. Stubborn bastard. And he leaves us to deal with all the
mess, eh.

The two women with the big rucksacks are standing behind the
pile of wood where the two herders are piling the last of the logs
in the dark. Is this Alp Prada, asks the woman with the silver
necklace, in standard German. Tired, they look tired. Like their
backs are hurting, and their heels sore. It's further back, that alp,
about another hour by foot. The two women look at each other.

In the clear alpine night, soldiers run in irregular pairs along
the dirt road. Their rifles are over their shoulders. Their buckles
clatter against the rifles. Officers run alongside them, like cam-
el drivers, quietly coaxing the soldiers with their rucksacks and
helmets. A second group rounds the bend after the first, then a
third. The farmhand, beside the cairn on the hill, holds on tight
to the dogs' collars till the fourth has also passed. You can hear
their boots on the dirt road.

At dawn, the swineherd comes out of the hut with his red milk
pails and goes across the yard towards the cowshed. He sees the
two women with the heavy rucksacks on the hay meadow be-

hind it, climbing over the fence. They cross the meadow to get to the dirt road, then vanish around the bend. The morning wind slams the barn door against the barn wall.

Linus's cow is lying, chained, in the cowshed. Chewing, she is, and the sound of her bell never varies. Ta-tac, ta-tac, ta-tac. The cowherd's on his stomach, along the spine of Linus's cow. He's resting his cheek on the cow's shoulder, one of his arms is down her side. Ta-tac, ta-tac, ta-tac. With the other hand, he's stroking her neck. His eyes close for moments at a time. Her hide's nice and warm.

How's it looking, the farmhand asks the hunter. The hunter raises his eyebrows. Just between us, he strokes his moustache, down there, in the woods, is a fine specimen, a major one. He fixes his hat and takes the kirsch from his inside pocket.

Gleiti entscheiva la battaglia. Sit tight for a few more days, then ding-ding, let battle commence, the dairyman says to the hunter, who is sitting in the parlor at the table beneath the big black bell. The clapper of the big bell is hanging, heavy, over his head. He has his hat on the table beside his cup. How's it looking, asks the dairyman, not so great, like every year, you know, doesn't really get any better, the hunter says. Stag hunting's a very recent thing, the hunter tries to claim. First stag was seen here in '29, people took it for a donkey. The dairyman nods. He knows this story, it's trotted out by the hunter every time he shows up.

Watch out for that hunter, the dairyman says, he has a forked tongue. The farmhand's standing beside him with the hammer in his hand. Between his lips are three nails. He hammers the nails into the wood of the wall. The dairyman doesn't look him in the eye. With the tip of his tongue, the farmhand tests the tips of the nails.

Inside the hut beside the door is the water tap with the concrete basin. It's a deep concrete basin. The dairyman pumps the whey from the cheese kettle into the basin. From the concrete basin, the pipes lead below ground to the pigs. Once the dairyman has started pumping the whey down, he calls across to the cowshed, pigs, a second time too, loud and clearly. Once all the whey's gone, the dairyman shouts into the pipe, that's me done, finito.

The tourist with the camera around his neck stops on the concrete step above the pig troughs. He's wearing a checked, short-sleeved shirt and an idiotic hat. The swineherd climbs into the pigpen with his two buckets of feed for the pigs. The pigs run up to the swineherd, him they know, and squeal and cry, pushing each other away. *Sooli, hohoo, hööila.* The swineherd has to push them aside with his boots. The tourist takes photos, turns to the hut, Margrit, he calls, Margrit. The swineherd pulls the first plug out. The tourist takes a photo. Margrit is filming. The whey runs into the trough. The swineherd goes across to the other side, puts his arm in the whey, up to above the elbow, and pulls the second plug out. The second trough begins to fill. The pigs push their way to the troughs, some have their hoofs in them. Did you catch that, are you filming, darling, the tourist says to his Margrit, in her knickerbockers and red walking socks. The swineherd wraps a bandage around the plug and crams it in the plughole so the pigs will have some left for the afternoon.

If Tumpiv has a hat on, good weather's on its way.

Fazandin's on a bough in a red fir, high above the ground, with the spade in his hand. Revive and delight the living spirits, fortify and warm your weak, cold brain, and quench your thirst, and quench your thirst, he sings, clinging to the trunk. Fazandin, Fazandin, climb down, get down from the tree, don't go falling off, thou owest death just one death.

The cowherd's squatting with his feet well apart, among the stones in a dried-up stream on the steep slope beneath Sez Ner, his trousers are down at his ankles. He's using one hand, the cowherd, to support himself on a stone. In the other, he has yellowed scraps of newspaper. The dogs sit patiently, on a stone at the edge of the stream, looking down into the valley.

Fog patches, like ultra-large sheets, move across the slopes of the Alps. The chimney of the hut on the neighboring alp has smoke coming from it. The dog's lying outside the hut beside the fountain. Lying in the fountain is the cowherd. She's stroking the dog's head. The washing on the clothesline blows in the wind.

The dairyman squeezes the teats. Slime as thick as butter drops onto the ground. The dairyman opens the packet with his teeth. He puts the syringe into the cow's teat and injects. A clean syringe for each teat. The cow kicks out with her leg, hoohhh. The cow slaps him around the ear with her tail.

When this is all over, the swineherd wants a donkey. It would have to be able to bend its ears backward and forward, to each side and all. It's a beautiful donkey, he wants, a really good one, an obstinate one. The donkey's name would be Gustav.

We've dried off a third of the cows, the dairyman says to his farmhand. The cows not giving milk go to Stavonas Sut and can just stay there. Arrange it with the two herders. They're off down there tomorrow. At midday, the herders and the farmhand carry fence posts and wooden mallets from the cowshed down the slope. They disappear into the forest, in the direction of Stavonas Sut, while the dairyman sits in the parlor beneath the black cowbell with the heavy clapper, with a newly cut cheese to accompany his Chianti. Making cheese is tiring.

In the wall of the hut is a red isolator. A jacket and a rope are hanging on it. The jacket's covered in dust. The jacket's been hanging for weeks now on the isolator outside the hut.

Beside the fountain on the hills above the hut, the swineherd's head and hat emerge from the well. The cowherd's standing at the fountain, cleaning the fountain with the broom. Okay, you can turn it on now, the cowherd says, pushing the plug in the plughole. Lying among the alpenroses, just up from the fountain, are soldiers in their sweaty fatigues. Their rifles are at the ready, the helmets well down over their eyes. Here and there, other soldiers are on their backs among the flowers, their helmets not on their heads but in their hands, and full to the brim with mushrooms they raucously devour.

The anniversary will soon be celebrated.

The jay in the treetops lets out a screech. The sun burns down on the clearing. Antlers, including a crown antler, stick out of the tall grass. The flies fly off when the hunter grabs the rotting stag by its mighty antlers. Beetles crawl over the stag's head, climb out of its mouth and ears. The hunter kneels before the stag and cuts its head off. The stench catches the back of his throat, the sun is burning the back of his neck.

The dry cows are herded onto Stavonas Sut, the pastures just down from the forest. The black ram trots along with the cows. The ram can stay with the cows, it'll be fine down there, the farmhand says. After all, it was well again now and enjoyed running around and eating and shitting. The ram trots along beside Giachen's cow. The dark one.

Below Sez Ner, the cows are beside the ski lift, far apart on the slopes. Over the fence, the flat-sounding bells of the heifers are climbing higher and higher up the slopes, as far as Sez Ner. The cowherd in charge of the heifers is lying next to the fence, in the alpenroses with her dog, eating an apple. Sitting beside her is the farmhand, putting his shoes on.

The dirt gets under your nails. The dirt stains your hands. The swineherd uses the boot-brush to try and get his hands clean. The dirt sticks in the folds, like it was etched there. The dirt only goes once the skin begins to peel. The skin begins to peel when the summer's over, as if your body was shedding its skin like a snake.

The farmhand's at the pigpen with the binoculars. He's looking across at Alp Titschal, on the other side of the side valley. Below the hut on Alp Titschal, the soldiers have set up camp. Five camouflage tents are among the cows on the slope. Below Péz Titschal, soldiers are visible with all kinds of equipment. They run around the slopes firing projectiles that detonate with a loud bang in the mountain, firing projectile after projectile into the mountain, as if they'd to strip the mountain by Sunday. Outside the hut on Alp Titschal, people in uniform are standing around with their hands on their hips. Others look up at the mountain, through binoculars. Beside the soldiers are two men in bright aprons and three farmers. They're gesticulating, pointing down, one minute, to the camp that has been set up on the cow pasture, and up at the mountain, the next. Below the hut, military vehicles are parked at the edge of the forest. The military vehicles are covered with camouflage tarps. The pigs, we should lock them up, the farmhand says to the swineherd. He hands him the binoculars and lights a Select.

Taking regular steps, the cowherd from the neighboring alp is climbing up to Sez Ner. Her hands are on her thighs as she takes each step. She doesn't look up till she reaches the cairn. On one side of the cairn is the iron signpost with the yellow signs. On the other, the iron cross. Standing and lying around the cross, are mountaineers and mountain people. The cowherd looks down the other side to Val Lumnezia. The villages are at different heights on the slopes. At the entrance to the valley, Cumbel. Then Morissen and Vella, which has two churches, and where the women sit on the right, and not the men.

On the steep slope, two young men are carrying their mountain bikes, along the perimeter fence between Alp Stavonas and Alp Prada. They've their helmets on their heads and are wearing bike shoes, the full kit. From time to time they stop, put their bikes down in the alpenroses, drink from bidons, then chop-chop, it's up onto their shoulders with their two-wheeled steeds again, to continue up the slopes till they reach the peak, where a group of Japanese is standing around a guide and her small red flag with a white cross. The bikers carry their bikes down the steep slope into Val Lumnezia. They get smaller and smaller, the further down they go. Beneath Sez Ner, on the Lugnez side, and in the evening shadows, is Alp Sezner.

The first woodpile has toppled. The dairyman's standing at the corner of the hut, with the broom from the cowshed. He positions the broomstick behind the second woodpile and gives it a push. These aren't what I'd call woodpiles, all it takes is a bit of wind to come along, to topple them, he says with a strangled voice, pushing on the broomstick. He pushes some more and pushes some more and pushes some more until the second woodpile also topples.

It's time for their voluntary work on the alp and the farmers are sitting around the table in the hut, slurping coffees with gentian schnapps in them. The rain is beating against the windows. The fog is lying low. In the warmth of the parlor, steam's coming off the wet farmers, as they sit beneath the black cowbell that hangs in the corner above the table next to the crucifix with the fir twig. *Killing of the Schweinhings*, the dairyman says, when the swineherd delivers a full jug of coffee to the warm parlor. The farmers smirk behind their beards. Their elbows are bunched together on the table and their heads lean forward. Sitting there like hunchbacks, they draw on their pipes and Brissagos. I'll be deducting the two pigs from your pay, the dairyman says. The farmers move their heads closer together, like tortoises.

The cheese cellar is the soul of a dairy alp, the dairyman says. Wheels of cheese are stored like gold ingots in the cheese cellar. The cheese cellar shows you how virile a dairyman is, his farmhand says. A dairyman without a cheese cellar is like a shepherd without a dog. The cowherd knows how fond the dairyman is of his cheese cellar. The dairyman sleeps with one eye open.

On Alp Titschal, the dairyman has fucked off and his farmhand has too, a farmer says, fucked off overnight, they did, *furtibus*. Come morning, the herders were standing there, helpless, as if someone had pinched their trousers, and no fuckin sign of the two musketeers. There's nothing else for it: a few farmers will just have to go up to the alp, and take turns, it being impossible to get staff at the height of summer. Not exactly surprising, is it, another farmer says, gesticulating wildly, with all the shenanigans that are going on, the soldiers outnumber the cows over there, one behind every stone, there is, no wonder the herdsmen decided to cut and run. Cowards is what they are, the dairyman says, the boss never cuts and runs, oldest rule in the book, that is, likes of them should be strung up in the village square. As if we hadn't enough to do in the fields, the farmer says, you're in a fix, sure enough, if the maggots have got to the staff on the alp even, not one bit funny, that is.

The morning sun is high in the sky. The pigs at the pig troughs are squealing and pushing and shoving each other, like they're afraid of going hungry. They plunge their snouts up to their eyes in the whey. Clemens is standing on the plinth above the pig troughs, looking through his binoculars, across to the other side, where the helicopter's flying the parts for the new chair lift up to the slopes. I was a skiing instructor for years, he says to the swineherd, I could still show these young pig-catchers a thing or two. Over thirty years I was, a skiing instructor for over thirty years. Over there, in Flims, he'd done his instructing, tourists from all over the world, he'd had, the Mericanas were his favorites though. He'd had a lot of Mericanas. The Mericanas had liked Clemens. Six languages, he can speak, he says. He lowers his binoculars again and looks at the swineherd. Rhaeto-Romanic, German, Italian, French, English, and Drivel. But it's Mericana he speaks. The swineherd pushes away the pigs tugging at his trousers and walks back to the hut with Clemens and the two empty plastic buckets. *Lu tgau ti*, Clemens says, he has to go now, a lot still to do, load of fuckin shit, all of it.

Lie too much and you'll grow horns, the dairyman tells the swineherd. It was best not even to start with the whole horn thing, exactly the same as with cows, it was. Once you have horns, they're a bastard to get rid of. St Peter up at the Gates, anyhow, wasn't fond of horns. He only lets people with no horns in, or people with just little horns.

Above the parlor table hangs the crucifix with the dry fir twig. In the corner, above the table, hangs the black cowbell with the heavy clapper. Around the parlor table sit the herdsmen. Their heads are down on the table and they're sleeping. It was a short night. The cows got out twice and wouldn't settle. The animals behaved like the ghosts were tormenting them. The animals weren't going to settle at all. Now all is calm, all is quiet. A fly's buzzing around the heads of the herdsmen.

The delegation of farmers reverses the Aebi up towards the entrance of the hut. The dairyman is in the doorway, with his hands in his pockets. He's put his white apron on. *Bien di*, says a farmer, holding his hand out to the dairyman. The dairyman doesn't take it. The farmer crosses the threshold, goes past the cheese kettle and into the parlor. The second farmer prepares everything in the back of the Aebi, let's go disco, greets the dairyman, and enters the hut. Wheel after wheel passes the dairyman in the doorway and is gobbled up by the Aebi, till the cheese cellar's finally empty.

From the forest beside the stream emerges a man, stripped to the waist. He's carrying a board on his back, the size of a parlor door. He's tied the board around his sweaty upper body with two ropes. The man is tied to the board. The ropes bite into the man's skin. He walks along the stream on the steep slope, in the direction of Sez Ner. He walks slowly. He doesn't stumble.

The swineherd has a rash. With every step he takes, between his balls and his thigh is in agony. Persistent, the rash is. It's like it has teeth, teeth made of broken fuckin glass.

On the slopes below Sez Ner is the man, stripped to the waist, drawing stones. He has drawn huge stones on his board. You just can't fathom these ertists, the dairyman says. Nothing better to do, they have, than force themselves up slopes with boards the size of a barn door, and then draw fuckin stones. If he'd draw a proper mountain at least, you could understand it, not the likes of this though.

The striped straw mattresses are lying across old pieces of furniture and the rubbish. The fire eats into the mattresses. The petrol can's where she left it, in the grass, two dozen paces from the flames. The flames rise into the evening sky, while the cowherd from the neighboring alp and the farmhand lie up in the hayloft in the barn. Autumn is just around the corner.

The dry cows are in the shade at the edge of the pasture beneath the firs. The cows slap their tails like brooms across their backs, the gnats and flies fly off, then land back on the cows' backs until the next slap with a tail. The cows shake their heads, the bell tongues hit against the bells, and the flies leave the cows in peace for a few moments. The farmhand strokes the cows' backs. He applies thick layers of milking grease to the teats, where the flies and the horseflies suck blood from the wounds. The cows scratch their udders with their hoofs. The black ram's lying next to Giachen's cow, the dark one. The ram's always close to the dark cow, the farmhand says, the dark cow tolerates the ram. She knows the ram eats less than she does. He knocks his hat right back with his three fingers and strokes the ram's forehead. The ram takes the farmhand's fingers in its mouth.

The egg in his trouser pocket breaks. The swineherd hears the shell crack and can feel the liquid on his thigh. The liquid runs down his leg and into his boot. He takes the shell from his trouser pocket and throws it to the chickens.

Otto and Vicki look at each other. They grin behind their beards. Otto is him, one of them says to the cowherd. The other one says, Otto is him. The cowherd can't tell the difference between them. The dairyman says Otto was born with a caul and Vicki is a stargazer, that's the difference.

The dairyman's at the window of his room upstairs, his hands leaning on the windowsill. On the windowsill are geraniums, the height of microphones. The fuckin pigs aren't fat enough, the dairyman says. The swineherd looks up at the dairyman. He has his hat at the back of his neck and the manure shovel in his hand. The dope runs around the swineherd with his tongue hanging out and pushes his nose between his legs. See to it that the pigs don't escape. But you don't hear me, do you, you numb-skull, your ears are full of shit. The dope paws at the swine-herd's trouser leg. The swineherd turns away from the window and goes to the pigpen. They're running around far too much, the dairyman calls after him. They're not meant to run around, they'll never fatten up if they do, it's not racing pigs we're breed-ing, they've to stay in the pen and get nice and fat, that's what they're there for, *capiu*.

The cows' tails, you could use to make wigs. Their teeth, to make buttons, and their hide for leather jackets. Their udders for an-ti-ageing creams, and their horns for bottle openers. The udders, also, to make fancy gloves, and the tongues, to make handbags. The hoofs, to make shoehorns. What's left would be fodder for the pigs.

The blue gas cylinder hangs from the ceiling in the parlor on the cow chain. It falls down suddenly when Georg's beneath the light. The bottom of the cylinder knocks Georg's Brissago from his gob and slices cleanly through his cup. A pale Georg stands in the parlor, with his finger through the handle of half a tea-cup. Before him on the floor, the blue gas cylinder in the pud-dle of coffee at the feet of the band of farmers, sitting unmoved on their posteriors, their gobs wide open as if God himself was behind all this.

The farmhand's in the parlor, tacking the postcard next to the antlers, beneath the other two that have been on the wall for weeks. On the front of the card, the little seaside town in the evening light. The sun is just above the horizon, at the edge of the postcard. At the bottom of the card, in colorful letters: *Saludos de España*. The swineherd takes the card off the wall. He reads it, just as he's read the others already, and hangs it back on the wall. He makes sure he puts the tack through the right place on the card.

Dark clouds have gathered in the sky. There is thunder. Lightning flashes down. In the grass, where the fence ends, lie the wooden posts, the bucket with the isolators, the reel of wire, the wooden mallets. The two herders shelter behind a hill as the thunderstorm tears through the valley and it starts to hail.

Georg has shot himself in the foot, says Giachen, peppering the back of his hand with snuff. Wanting to finish a rabbit off with a double-barreled shotgun, he was, instead of—crunch—just breaking the brute's neck. Giachen sniffs the snuff, whoa, wipes his nose with his sleeve. Got the rabbit by the ears, he did, trapped it between his knees, the gun behind its ears, and bang. He takes out his snot-rag, Giachen. Rabbit got a surprise and all.

The pig is staggering. The pig falls down. The pig has been given beer. At first it didn't want to, then it drank the whole bottle. The pig gets up, then falls down again.

Now the wolf's roaming our forests again, Gieri Blut says, we should really take advantage of it. We've not been able to catch the crafty bastard and even if we did, making schnitzel with it and selling them at a high price probably wouldn't do the trick either. Who'd eat it, nowadays people eat only what's made in a lab, almost. Still, instead of farming and getting a crooked back, we should go after the wolf. Collect its fuckin shit and can it, put a nice label with an amazing picture on it, right, and sell it to the museums for lots of money. That, in principle, was what those ertists would do. You'd say goodbye to your mucking-out boots and working in stony fields, telling you.

Gaudenz's cow was born in the wrong body. Her shoulder height is clearly above that of the others, and her rump with the docked tail, too broad for a Braunvieh. Her forehead is too low, and head too broad. The ears, on the other hand, are too small. She's more of a bull than a cow, the dairyman says, and she's aggressive and all. That's what will win her the garland for *pugniera*, the strongest cow, like every other year.

When it rains, the cows shit better, says Giosch. Clemens laughs.

The farmhand's sitting on the terrace of Restaurant Wali with a Calanda in front of him. The Calanda is lukewarm. The farmhand has crossed his feet on a chair and is looking up at the summit. The chairlifts are climbing the mountain. The waitress, in traditional costume, carries the nicely presented plates from the restaurant to the customers on the terrace. In the card rack on the doorframe are postcards with mountains on them, and valleys and cows and geraniums, a franc apiece. From the terrace, the farmhand can see how the wind forces the sack of potatoes that is the dairyman off from the restaurant, on his paraglider. Another beer please, the farmhand says. The storm clouds are hanging low in the upper Surselva and drifting slowly down the valley. The flags on the poles outside the restaurant flutter in the wind.

Otto and Vicki's uncle remained in his hamlet, right at the end of the valley, all his life, Gieri Blut says. Not once, it seems, did he leave the hamlet. Until, that is—and he was over sixty at that point—he went up the mountain in his own backyard and looked across the valleys and mountains. There was no end to his amazement. Wow, the world's a big place, isn't it, he said—it's said.

At the summit of Sez Ner is the cairn. The Stone Man. In the Stone Man's stomach is the book.

A man's sitting on the terrace of the mountain restaurant. In his hand, he has a postcard. It really is beautiful in the mountains, he says. In the mountains it's, eh, beautiful, his wife says, cleaning her glasses. Herr Schlüssel said that too. That it's beautiful in the mountains.

Things were different in the past. He wouldn't travel to Glion, where you'd to put a tie on and sit on leather seats. Things were different in the past. In the bar, you could get a beer for two-fifty. And if you went upstairs, it cost fifty-two-fifty.

The gray dog has lost its discs. The discs were fastened to its collar. The discs looked like medals. A medal for every year on the alp.

The dairyman's at the window in the parlor, turning the dial of the radio with the bent aerial. Static, gold in the Surselva, static, continues to turn, static, tests have shown, static, sold abroad, static. There it is, the fuckin mutt. He knocks the radio off, leaves the parlor, and slams the door. From the window of the parlor, the farmhand can see the dope running off. The dairyman walks with the spade through the puddles to the pigpen. He stops and leans on the spade. The handle is under his armpit.

After milking in the evening, the herders are behind the cow-shed. The swineherd's sitting on the bale of straw with his back against the wall of the shed. In his hand, he has a stone. The cowherd's sitting on the concrete step, stroking the tabby's fur. They hear the dope yelp, then a second time. When they reach the back of the hut, the spade's against the woodpile.

The tourist asks the swineherd, could he move a bit further forward, to be in the picture too. Could he move a bit closer to the pigs, as far forward as possible, as close as possible to the pigs, maybe just pet one on the head too, or on the back, then he could take a photo of him and the pigs before the mountain backdrop, and that would be really nice.

The farmhand's reading his book. A few decades ago, our Romansh parishes, with only a few exceptions, were farming communities, it says in the book, and now that has changed. The wind sweeps across the pigs' backs. There's not a cloud in the sky. The farmhand continues to browse. The terrible accident last year on the alp of Andiast, when lightning killed the dairyman and 14 cows, was a warning to us once again that we should beseech our Almighty Lord annually to protect our alps from disaster.

The cowherd's standing at the table in the parlor, cutting onions. The onions make his eyes sting. Behind him, Toni Liung and the dairyman are standing at the dresser beside the door. Toni Liung has a black phone, the size of a loaf of dark bread, in his hand. A *Natel B*, is what you call this model, he tells the dairyman, who is standing beside him with his hands on his hips, looking at the phone. You can make a two-minute call with it, Toni Liung says, so you don't have to drive down to the village any time something comes up. Quite practical, it is.

The farmhand's sitting on the toilet with a letter in his hand. The envelope with the foreign stamp is lying on the floor. When the farmhand needs to think, he likes to sit on the toilet. He rereads the letter from abroad.

The phone lies on the dresser for four weeks without a peep out of it. Toni Liung drops by three times, says he doesn't understand, either, why the damn thing isn't working, unscrews this and that, adjusts something, screws it back, there, it should work now. The phone's in the muck outside the hut. It stays there till summer is over.

Alp Nova, that's a modern alp, the dairyman says. They've connecting pipes, the milk goes directly from the milking machine to the cheese kettle. Three of us could manage the alp, he says to the farmhand, who doesn't look up. One to clean the sheds and the yard, go with the cows, put the fences up, a proper herder who is also able to milk. He stuffs spoonful after spoonful of milk pudding in his mouth. And the two of us in the hut. It's a modern alp, this Alp Nova. Not like here where you need people to carry the milk and every other day, they drop shit in it. Connecting pipes are classy. I'd make cheese, you'd do the rest.

The dairyman has blood on his shoes.

Right at the back of the cowshed is Gieri Blut's cow. She has mighty horns, beautifully formed, broad at the base, the biggest, perhaps, in the herd. She has an udder that's big and heavy, that almost touches the ground, that brushes the stalks of the withered alpenroses when she moves. A beauty of a beast, the farmhand says, when you see her from a distance, crossing the yard. A *Grande Dame*. A pleasure, it is, each time she turns up to carry the big bell across the yard, her nose high in the air. He rubs his palm the length of her stomach. A textbook cow, he says. If it wasn't for the milk, you don't get a great deal of milk out of her, two coffee cups full a day maybe, no more than that.

The marmots whistle and vanish into their holes. The wind carries their whistles across the slopes. High above, the buzzard is circling. The hunter's lying in wait behind the hills. Marmot oil is pure medicine, Giosch says, you can't beat it. Marmot oil, he says, is so fine, it goes right through your hand.

The dairyman from Alp Prada, a tall, lanky man, takes a piece of cheese into the parlor. Outside, night has started falling, the cowbells can be heard in the distance. On the table, candles are burning. Outside the hut, there's a fire. The farmhand and the herders are sitting around the fire with the herdsmen from Alp Prada, who pass around the bottles and roll cigarettes more than they speak. You came after all, the dairyman from Prada says to the dairyman, the guys from Alp Naul and Alp Nova are coming too. The dairyman cuts off a bit of cheese, bites into it, nods, while the dairyman from Prada hands him a cold bottle of beer he chilled in the fountain.

The swineherd's sitting with the other herdsmen around the fire outside the hut. The herdsmen from Alp Prada speak standard German and hand the swineherd the roll-up. The weed catches his throat and tastes sweetish. The swineherd's teeth feel so heavy. And that gives him a headache. The heavy teeth must be the cause of the headache. White elephants rise from the chimney.

Fazandin's standing near the herd, on Sez Ner. He has leaned his spade against the cairn. The fog is slowly breaking up. Fazandin stands on a stone beside the cross. His arms are stretched above his head and he's holding a stone bigger than his head.

The handle of the manure shovel has snapped. Alig drove over it with the Rapid. You can still see the marks on the bits of shaft. The cowherd sticks it together again, with insulating tape. It's the cowherd's fault, Alig tells the dairyman. It's Alig's fault, the cowherd tells the dog.

Dr. Stössel's coming, the farmhand says. Dr. Stössel drives a Porsche. You can hear him long before he rounds the bend. He races like a rocket, up the dirt road, then through to behind the hut. Dr. Stössel lives down at the bottom of the valley, in the forest. His house is a bit remote. All that's known about him is that he's a retired doctor from the lowland and drives a Porsche. The hunters don't like Stössel. In the hunting season, he creeps through the forest and disturbs the hunters. Nearly had a fuckin heart attack, I did, the hunter says. Down in the forest, it was. Stössel suddenly just rose from the mud in front of the boy, it seems. Thought Old Nick had come to get him personally, the boy did, seeing the gray beard and bush of gray hair on Dr. Stössel's chest. Naked, he was, and covered in mud, and he stood there, roaring like a stag, it seems. Hunter had left his binoculars lying in the thingamabob, he realized later. Three hundred plus, he'd paid for them.

In the hay barn, next to the hayloft, is a wooden crate. A herder would fit in the crate. The crate is locked with a lock. You can't open the lock, the two herders have tried and tried. Painted on the crate is the number forty-one, in black. Two dogs could fit in the crate, or a herder.

The hose at the cowshed has five holes in it. The holes are the width of blades of grass. The water pushes through the holes. By the autumn, the water drips through the holes. In the autumn, the jet from the hose is weak. The dairyman won't turn the wa-

ter tap on for the cowshed. We've hardly enough water in the
hut ourselves as it is, he says. In the autumn, water is scarce, the
brooms are done, the bristles on the brushes worn, and in the
shed, the muck clings to the rubber mats in the aisle. It's getting
worse every year, the dairyman says. No snow in the winter and
in the summer, no water. If it continues like this, we'll soon be
thinking it's Morocco we're in.

For the anniversary, everything will have to be immaculate, the
farmer from the delegation of farmers says. On Sunday, the live-
stock should stay in the pastures longer, if possible, so the guests
can celebrate undisturbed. He climbs over the fence beside the
cowshed and crosses the yard to the fountain. The dairyman
trots along behind, like a dog trained to do so. I'll see to it, the
dairyman says. The weather's supposed to be good again on Sunday, the farmer says when he gets to the plinth beside the pigpen. These guys though, these stink, and that's not on, natural-
ly, when important people are coming. They'll have to go. Hear
that, the dairyman says to the swineherd who is in among the
pigs and troughs with the two buckets of pig feed.

Behind the cowshed, on the mowed hay meadow, the farmers
are setting up the benches for the celebration. Four rows are put
out before the podium, where the speaker will speak. The flags
are hanging on the podium already: the Swiss flag, the flag of the
canton of Grisons, the flag of the commune. It's a clear morning,
not a cloud in the sky. The ding-dong ding-dong, you can hear
in the distance already.

Standing on the hill are the alphorn players. They've been invit-
ed up from the lowlands. Immaculately turned out, they stand
on the hill in their shining shoes, waiting. The cowbells are no
longer audible when the guests come around the bend. At the

front is the brass band, in uniform, then the Rapid and the Aebi, with the VIPs on the bridge. Behind the Aebi, the rest, all very jovial, all in traditional costume and pretty hats. At the first sight of the guests, the alphorn players from the lowlands start playing their alphorns. The bandleader at the front, beside the flag bearer whose forehead and upper lip are glistening with sweat, waves his baton to indicate *silencio*. The alphorn players, with their swollen cheeks and red faces, now send notes chasing across the meadows. The sun is beaming in the cloudless midday sky.

The rooster flies off when the bandleader jerks his baton and other hand, and the band blasts out the march, like they were firing it from a cannon, to the rhythm of Gieri Pign's big drum, who goads his colleagues in front of him, like it was cows he was goading. Beside Gieri Pign is Paul with his tuba and puffed-up cheeks and red face as he plays for the excited anniversary guests on the orange benches at the orange tables, with their big mugs of beer. Their noses and beards are all directed at the band in front of the raised podium at the entrance to the barn. The band lays into the music like life and death were at stake.

On the hill above the hut, the two herders are lying in their blue overalls and looking down at the anniversary guests, who are seated on the benches in front of the no-longer-straight podium, exercising their beer arms. The band's instruments are lying in the grass beside the fence, and shining in the evening sun. The pigs are nudging their way under the tables, eating the scraps that were dropped. The chickens, too, are in and about the guests. The goat tugs at the red flag in front of the podium, where the tabby's now sitting.

The pastures below Sez Ner are now grazed bare, the alpenroses have long since withered, the hills are a brownish color. The rough tongues of the cows, in this pasture one day, in the other another, are tearing any last grass out. Hunger forces the cows to break through the perimeter fence, down into the pastures below the alp, where the grass is taller than it is on it. Not even the electric fence can stop them, not whatever blessings they've had, and not the farmers' curses either.

The farmhand's lying with his book on the hill just up from the hut. Beside the farmhand is the cairn. Point one (he reads in the book): Precisely these Christian regions should be a home from home to people with a serious need and desire for tranquility. Point two: Visitors, for whom our region serves as a health resort, must never be given reason to take umbrage. Good personal relations make also the best economic sense in the long term. Point three: The village policemen must be permitted to intervene when a woman dresses inappropriately. Point four: In the event of bad weather, our guests should have access to suitable books and Christian newspapers in our public libraries.

That's not acceptable, the dairyman says to the farmhand. Fridolin's cow is not going to be declared the *miseriera*, the best dairy cow on the alp, believe me. He didn't care if the monthly records showed she produced more milk than all the others. She wasn't getting the biggest garland on the final day of the season. The farmhand touches the edge of his cap, in salute. That thing of Fridolin's always turned up looking like she came from the back of beyond. Plus, she's got a lousy little bell, and the best dairy cow also has to look the part. He spits on the ground. I've sorted this out with Giachen already.

Gion's trumpet is hanging on the milk scales. It weighs 3.2 kilos. Gion left his trumpet behind on Sunday and the cows walked all over it and dragged it up to outside the hut. On Sunday, it didn't have any dents and wasn't all twisted.

The pastures on Stavonas Sut will soon be grazed bare, the dairy-man says. We should really have horses in the pastures now, or sheep, they can mow shorter than the cows. Let hungry sheep or hungry horses into a pasture and by the time they're finished, it will look as neat as a golf course. Cows can't do that.

A little marmot oil from time to time, Linus says, stroking the neck of his old cow, then stroking her nose. Linus doesn't say a lot. He's patience personified, the farmhand says, as patient as a tree stump. The cow takes Linus's hand in her mouth. Her tongue's as smooth as the tongue of any calf.

The dairyman's behind the cowshed on his stomach. He's firing, bang, his Flobert gun, bang, at the target on the barn door. His legs are apart and his elbows, propped on the ground. The dairy-man is breathing regularly and holds his breath before he pulls the trigger. The barrel of the Flobert rises slightly after each shot. Thin smoke comes out of the barrel.

The wire's all tangled. The swineherd tries to untangle the wire. He has the impression the whole thing just gets more and more tangled, the more he pulls at it. At some point, he throws the bundle of wire on the ground. He lifts it again and tries some more. For however long it takes him to untangle this, he won't be able to finish the perimeter fence.

On the inside of the cupboard door, the sizes of the herds in recent years are noted in pencil. The number of cattle has re-mained constant. Beneath the dates are the names of all the herdsmen. On Sunday, Giachen told them all how the previous dairyman, who did nearly fifteen years in a row on the alp, had been a useless so-and-so, totally useless, a bit much his crumbly cheese had been, a damn cheek you'd have needed to try and sell it. At least his wife had been good on the alp. Whereas that old so-and-so would lie, day in, day out, on two old mattresses in the parlor. Completely legless, needless to say. His wife had had to do all the work, and his sons.

The dairyman's no longer making cheese every day. Nearly a third of the cows have been dried off and are now in the pastures at Stavonas Sut. They're waiting to be taken back down to the village. The first cows will calve at the start of October already. After breakfast, the dairyman covers the cheese kettle until more milk comes. To make cheese once it's worth it, he says. Meanwhile, on good days, he takes a seat on the wooden bench with the engraved plaque outside the hut, or drives his Justy down to the village and comes up again in the evening or the following day.

The tarot cards are lying on the table. People often play tarot in the valley. The children play *Mund sutsu*, upside-down world, with the same cards. The strongest card is the World. The weakest card is the Bagat. The Bagat looks like a chicken keeper. The swineherd lays the cards out on the parlor table. The World can only be beaten by the Bagat. The Bagat is actually the strongest card.

By the end of the summer, the soles of their boots are worn thin and their boots are as comfy as house shoes.

The swineherd is mopping the floors. The water in the metal bucket is dark gray. He wipes the floors with the floor cloth. At certain bits, the dirt sticks to the floor. As he scrubs the floor, the swineherd thinks about the dream he had last night. Last night, he bit through his specs. He's amazed, not because he bit through his specs but because he doesn't wear specs. He doesn't need specs. The swineherd has the vision of a hunter. He has eyes of flint.

The dairyman wants to go to Alp Nova. The farmhand wants away, and the swineherd wants a large portion of fries with a big fat breaded schnitzel, the size of the sole of his boot, with ketchup, a slice of lemon, and for dessert, an ice-cream sundae, a Coupe Käthi.

The fir is swaying. *Attenzium, plonta sederscha*, the man with a rattling chainsaw in his hand shouts and takes a few steps back. The fir topples. Its branches brush against the other trees. The trunk snaps completely and the fir falls on the dirt road. The chainsaws start to rattle again. The men get to work on the fir, from all sides. The chainsaws bite through the fir and spit the sawdust all over the road. Here, in the middle of the forest, is where the new road will go, from the villages up to Stavonas Sut. Things haven't got that far yet, and the chainsaws aren't about to tire.

In the middle of the road, after the last gully before the border of the alp, is a stone. The stone's as broad as the road and the height of a herder. The stone lies there, in the middle of the road, like it fell to earth.

In the middle of the clearing in the forest are two naked people. Their rucksacks and sticks are lying close to their heads. They don't notice the cowherd. The cowherd from the neighboring alp is lying on the farmhand, her hands are pressing on his chest. Her eyes are closed. She's smiling. The cowherd clears off into the forest. The two of them, presumably, haven't seen Clemens's cows either.

The dairyman is whistling folk songs. He's had news from the inspectors. The dairyman's whistling as he milks the cows in the evening. He's still whistling the next day as he makes cheese.

Giosch is as fond of his cow as the dairyman is of his cheese cellar. When the time comes, Giosch will have his cow stuffed and keep it in the parlor, the dairyman says. A cow like that comes along just once in every fifty years, Giosch tells the farmhand. Cows like that are rare. They don't grow behind a rock.

The two herders are on the hill below Sez Ner, throwing stones at the sign for a ski slope. The yellow sign on the red signpost is lying across the cattle tracks. The sign answers when a stone hits it. The stones trace a large arc in the air. The cowherd's leading 3-2. Four stones remain. After that, it's sudden death until a winner emerges, and also a loser, who will have to climb Sez Ner and collect the fence posts.

The farmhand's sitting on the bench outside the hut, shaving. Beside the farmhand on the bench is a basin with water. Steam is coming off the water in the basin. The farmhand has a piece of a mirror in his hand. His razor's making only difficult progress with the beard. Shaving foam is clinging to the farmhand's throat and ears. He has cut himself. A trail of blood from the cut is running down his cheek.

She made the Schabziger, the cowherd from the neighboring alp. Delicious. Luis hands the cowherd a bit. He takes out a small bottle and two glasses and pours the drinks. Every now and then, he looks in on the neighboring alp to check everything's okay. The old herdsman on that alp was half-decomposed when they found him, years ago now too, already. He looked terrible, Luis says. I helped to retrieve and bury him. In the village they then complained because we buried the herdsman, the victim of an accident, in a coffin made of un-planed timber. He pours more, fills the glasses right up. They didn't want to bury him themselves, needless to say. He didn't go to church, you see, but complain, aye, they could do that all right. They clink glasses. Really excellent, the Schabziger.

Toni Liung herds the last pig onto the Aebi and closes the tailgate. The pigs have been squeezed in tight. They squeal like they know why they're in there. Now it doesn't matter whether they've nose rings or not, the butcher in the village isn't interested.

Linus's old cow, bring her back up from Stavonas Sut today, the dairyman says. Linus is coming with the Rapid to fetch her. She'll be calving soon, a cash cow, she is, Luis's old cow, calves more than other cows wouldn't even in two lives. He cuts a bit of bread off. Get me some butter, he says to the cowherd, make sure it's fresh, straight from the churn. Luis is a lucky so-and-so. He has *in nas fin*, a good nose, for everything he takes it into his head to do. The cowherd puts the plate with fresh butter down on the table. He bumps his head against the antlers. The antlers wobble but don't fall. That's the twenty-second calf his old cow has produced, she just keeps calving, doesn't want to die. The farmhand dunks a bit of bread in his white coffee. When he fetches Linus's cow though, he's to leave the dog here and kindly not chase the cow back up. She's not the youngest any more after all, and we've had enough stillborn calves as it is, *zaffermustas*.

Giachen's standing on the plinth beside the pigpen, and looking down on the profiles that are put up in summer. They want to build a hotel up the middle of the valley. Some guy from who-knows-where has bought up *rubas e schrubas*, everything and anything. He also wants to build an indoor ski slope so they can ski all year round, in winter and in summer. And the *cuac* who is building this monster has now bought Tumpiv and all. It won't be long, presumably, before Tumpiv is being renamed or demolished, or at least has its peak removed so they can get their helicopter up on it and sip their bubbly there. You can forget your tranquility then, eh.

The coffee's as thin as cow piss. They're short on coffee now and what coffee there is has to last for the days that remain. Every additional expenditure will mean less pay for the herdsmen. Put like that, it's fine for the coffee to be thinner. For the swineherd and the cowherd, there's none at all now. You two can drink water, it's better for you anyhow, you'll end up being too fidgety otherwise, the dairyman says.

The milk inspector is in the parlor, standing with his back to the wall. His shock of white hair is bang in front of the antlers. The antlers are sticking out, either side of his head. Am I glad this is the final inspection. Having to climb up here every month, soon he won't want to anymore, he says. The farmers will need to find some other clown for next year.

You've still things to learn, the dairyman tells the swineherd. You won't make it to dairyman in this incarnation, I'd bet a calf on it. The one after next, maybe. Dairymen don't grow on trees, you're *born* a dairyman. Same goes for swineherds.

The swineherd's beside the cairn. The Stone Man. Apologies, the swineherd says, starting to take him apart. He takes stone after stone in his hands, examining them closely, like he's been asked to check their condition, and lays them all out, the big ones in one pile, the medium-sized, and the small ones, until the Stone Man has been dismantled. *Vualà*, he says, taking a stone slab, wiping it with his hand, and putting it down in the grass, where the Stone Man had stood. With a sharp stone, he scratches a symbol on the slab. The swineherd piles the stones on the slab, one by one, and with care, so the cairn will withstand all weathers till it's put back in place.

The salt gets through the fine cracks in the plastic gloves and onto his hands. The cowherd dips his hands in the whey to ease the sting. The dairyman comes into the cheese cellar and stands at the table with his hands on his hips. His breath stinks of strong brandy. He watches for a while, then leaves the cheese cellar, banging the door. The priest tried to explain to him at the anniversary do, the farmhand tells the cowherd, why you shouldn't drink alcohol without drinking to something first. With one hand, he turns the wheel of cheese around, in a circle. In the dim light of the cheese cellar, it looks like a misshapen consecrated wafer. Seems drinking to something, or rather: the clinking of glasses, banishes evil from the alcohol.

The dairyman's sitting on the bench outside the hut, holding the radio with the bent aerial. The Bishop of Chur wishes to employ an exorcist, they're saying on the radio. The swineherd's scratching his way across the yard with the manure shovel. Shoosh, the dairyman says. Nothing but static again, damn fuckin thing, the dairyman says. He turns the dial on the radio. Beside him on the bench is the yellowed *Blick* the farmers left in the parlor. The swineherd pushes the wheelbarrow with the missing arm across the yard and into the cowshed. The wheel on the wheelbarrow squeaks. The rooster's standing on the edge of the fountain, crowing.

Clemens, the stammerer, is back out of hospital, says Köbi. The rain's hammering on the window. The radio with the bent aerial is hissing again. He'd just spent a few weeks in hospital, Clemens, was in a bad way. The farmers nod. He was better now, seemingly, drinking like a horse at a trough, still. He'd a weakness when it came to schnapps, of course. They'd tried to get him, at the hospital, to give up smoking and all. He's smoking like a train again now, Giachen says. In the hospital, he'd gone round the ashtrays, smoked other people's butts. Now thought even less of men in white jackets and their pieces of wisdom, Clemens did. Not that it's exactly easy to kill Clemens. And that goes for Him-Up-There, Him-Down-Below, and the schnapps, too. *Smaledet zai*, he's a tough cookie, Clemens. The cowherd brings in a jug of hot coffee and the schnapps to put in it. He puts them down on the table. He was spending all day, every day, going from bar to bar again, Clemens. He'll enter the bar and give the barmaid the thumbs up, meaning he wants a *grosses Bier*.

What's happening with the goat, Giosch asks. Fucker can go and jump in the lake. The goat jumps down, off the edge of the fountain. It was a good goat, he'd take it, says Giosch. We'll see, says the dairyman, taking the blade of grass out of his mouth. There was a guy lived in the village once, been dead for a few years now, Giosch says, kept his goat chained up in the dark in the shed, all its life. He takes his Brissago out of his mouth. Seems everyone in the village knew, he takes his matches from his jacket pocket, but no one ever actually saw the goat.

The garlands to be presented before the official descent are on the table in the parlor. The garland for Best Dairy Cow, the *miseriera*, looks like a decorated milking stool. The garland for Strongest Cow, the *pugniera*, looks similar. They've gone to some trouble with the garlands, adding paper flowers, red and white, and sufficient fresh fir.

Morality is a frost, says Luis. And frost arrives early here, and stops late. The first frost burns any green shoots. It clears the hillside. What remains has always been there. You can depend on frost.

It's a cabaret, the farmhand says.

You're better holding your tongue, you numbskull, Giachen says to Gieri Blut. There was no reason to be afraid of getting a raw deal, the whole valley knew who had the big gong around here, it would pay to watch out. Gieri waves his fist, he wasn't going to be called a numbskull by anyone, right, did he want him to show him where God hangs out, a *tgigerlut*, a scaredy-cat, he was. You numbskull, wretched numbskull, Giachen shouts. Toni Liung now gets involved too, Köbi also, until Gieri takes Giachen by the ears.

Once they've been milked for the final time, the cowherd herds the cows out into the hay meadow, where the farmhand's standing beside the boxes of garlands and presenting the cows with garlands of varying sizes. The cows use the corner of the cowshed and the fence to try and rip the garlands off. By the time the farmhand and the cowherd have presented all the garlands, the valley is completely clouded over.

Behind the cowshed beside the wheelbarrow with the missing arm is the log. The log where justice is done. The swineherd holds the hen's legs tight and spins it in the air. The large axe flashes in the last of the sun. Chop. The headless chicken jumps onto the cattle tracks and over nearby hills and stones. You'd think it had just seen Death. Five more times, the axe smashes down on the log. The heads of six chickens lie in the blood around the log. One last hen remains. Chop. The rooster's now alone.

The farmers have brought along traditional shirts with flowery collars for the two herders. They put them on so that, down in the villages, the snouts of lenses can photograph them before the herd with all the garlands, with their sticks in their hands and their hats on their heads, well down over their foreheads. Down in the village, after the final procession, the two herders will give the delegation of farmers their traditional shirts back. Once the herd has arrived, the farmers will drink to the good summer. The two herders—adieu—will have long since vanished.

The herd sets off. Leading the pack are the cows with the large garlands, with the pretentious, extravagant bells the farmers brought up to the alp for them for the official descent. Bells bigger than bulls' heads they wish they could have worn themselves. Garland after garland wanders off down the slope, every last cow's neck with a snazzy garland around it. The rooster and the dairyman remain behind.

The rain gets heavier, the clouds have burst. Before the herd can reach the forest, it's raining like it rarely does here, two decades' worth, getting stronger and stronger as it passes over the cows' backs, the rain, as merciless, it lashes down on the alp, like it wanted to give the alp a good clean, like it wanted to take the slopes with it, the slopes, the cowshed, the hut, the whole she-bang, the entire circus.

MICHAL AJVAZ,
The Golden Age.
The Other City.
PIERRE ALBERT-BIROT,
Grabinoulor.
YUZ ALESHKOVSKY,
Kangaroo.
FELIPE ALFAU,
Chromos.
Locos.
IVAN ÂNGELO,
The Celebration.
The Tower of Glass.
ANTÓNIO LOBO ANTUNES,
Knowledge of Hell.
The Splendor of Portugal.
ALAIN ARIAS-MISSON,
Theatre of Incest.
JOHN ASHBERY & JAMES SCHUYLER,
A Nest of Ninnies.
ROBERT ASHLEY,
Perfect Lives.
GABRIELA AVIGUR-ROTEM,
Heatwave and Crazy Birds.
DJUNA BARNES,
Ladies Almanack.
Ryder.
JOHN BARTH,
Letters.
Sabbatical.
DONALD BARTHELME,
The King.
Paradise.
SVETISLAV BASARA,
Chinese Letter.
MIQUEL BAUÇÀ,
The Siege in the Room.
RENÉ BELLETTO,
Dying.
MAREK BIENCZYK,
Transparency.
ANDREI BITOV,
Pushkin House.

ANDREJ BLATNIK,
You Do Understand.
LOUIS PAUL BOON,
Chapel Road.
My Little War.
Summer in Termuren.
ROGER BOYLAN,
Killoyle.
IGNÁCIO DE LOYOLA BRANDÃO,
Zero.
Anonymous Celebrity.
BONNIE BREMSER,
Troia: Mexican Memoirs.
CHRISTINE BROOKE-ROSE,
Amalgamemnon.
BRIGID BROPHY,
In Transit.
GERALD L. BRUNS,
Modern Poetry and the Idea of Language.
GABRIELLE BURTON,
Heartbreak Hotel.
MICHEL BUTOR,
Degrees.
Mobile.
G. CABRERA INFANTE,
Infante's Inferno.
Three Trapped Tigers.
JULIETA CAMPOS,
The Fear of Losing Eurydice.
ANNE CARSON,
Eros the Bittersweet.
ORLY CASTEL-BLOOM,
Dolly City.
LOUIS-FERDINAND CÉLINE,
North.
Rigadoon.
Castle to Castle.
Conversations with Professor Y.
London Bridge.
Normance.
MARIE CHAIX,
The Laurels of Lake Constance.
HUGO CHARTERIS,
The Tide Is Right.

ERIC CHEVILLARD,
Demolishing Nisard.

MARC CHOLODENKO,
Mordechai Schamz.

JOSHUA COHEN,
Witz.

EMILY HOLMES COLEMAN,
The Shutter of Snow.

ROBERT COOVER,
A Night at the Movies.

STANLEY CRAWFORD,
Log of the S.S. The Mrs Unguentine.
Some Instructions to My Wife.

RENÉ CREVEL,
Putting My Foot in It.

RALPH CUSACK,
Cadenza.

NICHOLAS DELBANCO,
Sherbrookes.
The Count of Concord.

NIGEL DENNIS,
Cards of Identity.

PETER DIMOCK,
A Short Rhetoric for Leaving the Family.

ARIEL DORFMAN,
Konfidenz.

COLEMAN DOWELL,
Island People.
Too Much Flesh and Jabez.

ARKADII DRAGOMOSHCHENKO,
Dust.

RIKKI DUCORNET,
Phosphor in Dreamland.
The Complete Butcher's Tales.
The Jade Cabinet.
The Fountains of Neptune.

WILLIAM EASTLAKE,
The Bamboo Bed.
Castle Keep. Lyric of the Circle Heart.

JEAN ECHENOZ,
Chopin's Move.

STANLEY ELKIN,
A Bad Man.
Criers and Kibitzers, Kibitzers and Criers.
The Dick Gibson Show.

The Franchiser.
The Living End.
Mrs. Ted Bliss.

FRANÇOIS EMMANUEL,
Invitation to a Voyage.

SALVADOR ESPRIU,
Ariadne in the Grotesque Labyrinth.

LESLIE A. FIEDLER,
Love and Death in the American Novel.

JUAN FILLOY,
Op Oloop.

ANDY FITCH, *Pop Poetics.*

GUSTAVE FLAUBERT, *Bouvard and Pécuchet.*

KASS FLEISHER, *Talking out of School.*

JON FOSSE, *Aliss at the Fire. Melancholy.*

FORD MADOX FORD,
The March of Literature.

MAX FRISCH,
I'm Not Stiller.
Man in the Holocene.

CARLOS FUENTES,
Christopher Unborn.
Distant Relations.
Terra Nostra.
Where the Air Is Clear.

TAKEHIKO FUKUNAGA,
Flowers of Grass.

WILLIAM GADDIS, JR.,
The Recognitions.

JANICE GALLOWAY,
Foreign Parts.
The Trick Is to Keep Breathing.

WILLIAM H. GASS,
Cartesian Sonata and Other Novellas.
The Tunnel.
Willie Masters' Lonesome Wife.

GÉRARD GAVARRY,
Hoppla! 1 2 3.

ETIENNE GILSON,
The Arts of the Beautiful.
Forms and Substances in the Arts.

C. S. GISCOMBE,
Giscome Road.
Here.

DOUGLAS GLOVER,
Bad News of the Heart.

WITOLD GOMBROWICZ,
A Kind of Testament.

PAULO EMÍLIO SALES GOMES,
P's Three Women.

GEORGI GOSPODINOV,
Natural Novel.

JUAN GOYTISOLO,
Count Julian.
Juan the Landless.
Makbara.
Marks of Identity.

HENRY GREEN,
Back.
Blindness.
Concluding.
Doting.
Nothing.

JACK GREEN,
Fire the Bastards!

JIŘÍ GRUŠA,
The Questionnaire.

MELA HARTWIG,
Am I a Redundant Human Being?

JOHN HAWKES,
The Passion Artist.
Whistlejacket.

ELIZABETH HEIGHWAY, ED.,
Contemporary Georgian Fiction.

ALEKSANDAR HEMON, ED.,
Best European Fiction.

AIDAN HIGGINS,
Balcony of Europe.
Blind Man's Bluff.
Bornholm Night-Ferry.
Flotsam and Jetsam.
Langrishe, Go Down.
Scenes from a Receding Past.

KEIZO HINO,
Isle of Dreams.

KAZUSHI HOSAKA,
Plainsong.

ALDOUS HUXLEY,
Antic Hay.

Crome Yellow.
Point Counter Point.
Those Barren Leaves.
Time Must Have a Stop.

NAOYUKI II,
The Shadow of a Blue Cat.

GERT JONKE,
The Distant Sound.
Geometric Regional Novel.
Homage to Czerny.
The System of Vienna.

JACQUES JOUET,
Mountain R.
Savage.
Upstaged.

MIEKO KANAI,
The Word Book.

YORAM KANIUK,
Life on Sandpaper.

HUGH KENNER,
Flaubert.
Joyce and Beckett: The Stoic Comedians.
Joyce's Voices.

DANILO KIŠ,
The Attic.
Garden, Ashes.
The Lute and the Scars.
Psalm 44.
A Tomb for Boris Davidovich.

ANITA KONKKA,
A Fool's Paradise.

GEORGE KONRÁD,
The City Builder.

TADEUSZ KONWICKI,
A Minor Apocalypse.
The Polish Complex.

MENIS KOUMANDAREAS,
Koula.

ELAINE KRAF,
The Princess of 72nd Street.

JIM KRUSOE,
Iceland.

AYSE KULIN,
Farewell: A Mansion in Occupied Istanbul.

EMILIO LASCANO TEGUI,
On Elegance While Sleeping.

FOR A FULL LIST OF PUBLICATIONS, VISIT: www.dalkeyarchive.com

ERIC LAURRENT,
Do Not Touch.

VIOLETTE LEDUC,
La Bâtarde.

EDOUARD LEVÉ,
Autoportrait.
Suicide.

MARIO LEVI,
Istanbul Was a Fairy Tale.

DEBORAH LEVY,
Billy and Girl.

JOSÉ LEZAMA LIMA,
Paradiso.

ROSA LIKSOM,
Dark Paradise.

OSMAN LINS,
Avalovara.
The Queen of the Prisons of Greece.

ALF MAC LOCHLAINN,
Out of Focus.
The Corpus in the Library.

RON LOEWINSOHN,
Magnetic Field(s).

MINA LOY,
Stories and Essays of Mina Loy.

D. KEITH MANO,
Take Five.

MICHELINE AHARONIAN MARCOM,
The Mirror in the Well.

BEN MARCUS,
The Age of Wire and String.

WALLACE MARKFIELD,
Teitlebaum's Window.
To an Early Grave.

DAVID MARKSON,
Reader's Block.
Wittgenstein's Mistress.

CAROLE MASO,
AVA.

LADISLAV MATEJKA &
KRYSTYNA POMORSKA, EDS.,
Readings in Russian Poetics: Formalist
and Structuralist Views.

HARRY MATHEWS,
Cigarettes.

The Conversions.
The Human Country: New and Collected
Stories.
The Journalist.
My Life in CIA.
Singular Pleasures.
The Sinking of the Odradek.
Stadium.
Tlooth.

JOSEPH MCELROY,
Night Soul and Other Stories.

ABDELWAHAB MEDDEB,
Talismano.

GERHARD MEIER,
Isle of the Dead.

HERMAN MELVILLE,
The Confidence-Man.

AMANDA MICHALOPOULOU,
I'd Like.

STEVEN MILLHAUSER,
The Barnum Museum.
In the Penny Arcade.

RALPH J. MILLS, JR.,
Essays on Poetry.

MOMUS,
The Book of Jokes.

CHRISTINE MONTALBETTI,
The Origin of Man.
Western.

OLIVE MOORE,
Spleen.

NICHOLAS MOSLEY,
Accident.
Assassins.
Catastrophe Practice.
Experience and Religion.
A Garden of Trees.
Hopeful Monsters.
Imago Bird.
Impossible Object.
Inventing God.
Judith.
Look at the Dark.
Natalie Natalia.
Serpent.
Time at War.

FOR A FULL LIST OF PUBLICATIONS, VISIT: www.dalkeyarchive.com

WARREN MOTTE,
Fables of the Novel: French Fiction since 1990.
Fiction Now: The French Novel in the
21st Century.
Oulipo: A Primer of Potential Literature.

GERALD MURNANE,
Barley Patch.
Inland.

YVES NAVARRE,
Our Share of Time.
Sweet Tooth.

DOROTHY NELSON,
In Night's City.
Tar and Feathers.

ESHKOL NEVO,
Homesick.

WILFRIDO D. NOLLEDO,
But for the Lovers.

FLANN O'BRIEN,
At Swim-Two-Birds.
The Best of Myles.
The Dalkey Archive.
The Hard Life.
The Poor Mouth.
The Third Policeman.

CLAUDE OLLIER,
The Mise-en-Scène.
Wert and the Life Without End.

GIOVANNI ORELLI,
Walaschek's Dream.

PATRIK OUŘEDNÍK,
Europeana.
The Opportune Moment, 1855.

BORIS PAHOR,
Necropolis.

FERNANDO DEL PASO,
News from the Empire.
Palinuro of Mexico.

ROBERT PINGET,
The Inquisitory.
Mahu or The Material.
Trio.

MANUEL PUIG,
Betrayed by Rita Hayworth.
The Buenos Aires Affair.
Heartbreak Tango.

RAYMOND QUENEAU,
The Last Days.
Odile.
Pierrot Mon Ami.
Saint Glinglin.

ANN QUIN,
Berg.
Passages.
Three.
Tripticks.

ISHMAEL REED,
The Free-Lance Pallbearers.
The Last Days of Louisiana Red.
Ishmael Reed: The Plays.
Juice!
Reckless Eyeballing.
The Terrible Threes.
The Terrible Twos.
Yellow Back Radio Broke-Down.

JASIA REICHARDT,
15 Journeys Warsaw to London.

NOËLLE REVAZ,
With the Animals.

JOÃO UBALDO RIBEIRO,
House of the Fortunate Buddhas.

JEAN RICARDOU,
Place Names.

RAINER MARIA RILKE,
The Notebooks of Malte Laurids Brigge.

JULIÁN RÍOS,
The House of Ulysses.
Larva: A Midsummer Night's Babel.
Poundemonium.
Procession of Shadows.

AUGUSTO ROA BASTOS,
I the Supreme.

DANIËL ROBBERECHTS,
Arriving in Avignon.

JEAN ROLIN,
The Explosion of the Radiator Hose.

OLIVIER ROLIN,
Hotel Crystal.

ALIX CLEO ROUBAUD,
Alix's Journal.

FOR A FULL LIST OF PUBLICATIONS, VISIT: www.dalkeyarchive.com

JACQUES ROUBAUD,
The Form of a City Changes Faster, Alas, Than the Human Heart.
The Great Fire of London.
Hortense in Exile.
Hortense Is Abducted.
The Loop.
Mathematics: The Plurality of Worlds of Lewis.
The Princess Hoppy.
Some Thing Black.
RAYMOND ROUSSEL,
Impressions of Africa.
VEDRANA RUDAN,
Night.
STIG SÆTERBAKKEN,
Siamese.
Self Control.
LYDIE SALVAYRE,
The Company of Ghosts.
The Lecture.
The Power of Flies.
LUIS RAFAEL SÁNCHEZ,
Macho Camacho's Beat.
SEVERO SARDUY,
Cobra & Maitreya.
NATHALIE SARRAUTE,
Do You Hear Them?
Martereau.
The Planetarium.
ARNO SCHMIDT,
Collected Novellas.
Collected Stories.
Nobodaddy's Children.
Two Novels.
ASAF SCHURR,
Motti.
GAIL SCOTT,
My Paris.
DAMION SEARLS,
What We Were Doing and Where We Were Going.
JUNE AKERS SEESE,
Is This What Other Women Feel Too?
What Waiting Really Means.

BERNARD SHARE,
Inish.
Transit.
VIKTOR SHKLOVSKY,
Bowstring.
Knight's Move.
A Sentimental Journey: Memoirs 1917–1922.
Energy of Delusion: A Book on Plot.
Literature and Cinematography.
Theory of Prose.
Third Factory.
Zoo, or Letters Not about Love.
PIERRE SINIAC,
The Collaborators.
KJERSTI A. SKOMSVOLD,
The Faster I Walk, the Smaller I Am.
JOSEF ŠKVORECKÝ,
The Engineer of Human Souls.
GILBERT SORRENTINO,
Aberration of Starlight.
Blue Pastoral.
Crystal Vision.
Imaginative Qualities of Actual Things.
Mulligan Stew.
Pack of Lies.
Red the Fiend.
The Sky Changes.
Something Said.
Splendide-Hôtel.
Steelwork.
Under the Shadow.
W. M. SPACKMAN,
The Complete Fiction.
ANDRZEJ STASIUK,
Dukla.
Fado.
GERTRUDE STEIN,
The Making of Americans.
A Novel of Thank You.
LARS SVENDSEN,
A Philosophy of Evil.
PIOTR SZEWC,
Annihilation.
GONÇALO M. TAVARES,
Jerusalem.
Joseph Walser's Machine.
Learning to Pray in the Age of Technique.

LUCIAN DAN TEODOROVICI,
Our Circus Presents...

NIKANOR TERATOLOGEN,
Assisted Living.

STEFAN THEMERSON,
Hobson's Island.
The Mystery of the Sardine.
Tom Harris.

TAEKO TOMIOKA,
Building Waves.

JOHN TOOMEY,
Sleepwalker.

JEAN-PHILIPPE TOUSSAINT,
The Bathroom.
Camera.
Monsieur.
Reticence.
Running Away.
Self-Portrait Abroad.
Television.
The Truth about Marie.

DUMITRU TSEPENEAG,
Hotel Europa.
The Necessary Marriage.
Pigeon Post.
Vain Art of the Fugue.

ESTHER TUSQUETS,
Stranded.

DUBRAVKA UGRESIC,
Lend Me Your Character.
Thank You for Not Reading.

TOR ULVEN,
Replacement.

MATI UNT,
Brecht at Night.
Diary of a Blood Donor.
Things in the Night.

ÁLVARO URIBE & OLIVIA SEARS, EDS.,
Best of Contemporary Mexican Fiction.

ELOY URROZ,
Friction.
The Obstacles.

LUISA VALENZUELA,
Dark Desires and the Others.
He Who Searches.

PAUL VERHAEGHEN,
Omega Minor.

AGLAJA VETERANYI,
Why the Child Is Cooking in the Polenta.

BORIS VIAN,
Heartsnatcher.

LLORENÇ VILLALONGA,
The Dolls' Room.

TOOMAS VINT,
An Unending Landscape.

ORNELA VORPSI,
The Country Where No One Ever Dies.

AUSTRYN WAINHOUSE,
Hedyphagetica.

CURTIS WHITE,
America's Magic Mountain.
The Idea of Home.
Memories of My Father Watching TV.
Requiem.

DIANE WILLIAMS,
Excitability: Selected Stories.
Romancer Erector.

DOUGLAS WOOLF,
Wall to Wall.
Ya! & John-Juan.

JAY WRIGHT,
Polynomials and Pollen.
The Presentable Art of Reading Absence.

PHILIP WYLIE,
Generation of Vipers.

MARGUERITE YOUNG,
Angel in the Forest.
Miss MacIntosh, My Darling.

REYOUNG,
Unbabbling.

VLADO ŽABOT,
The Succubus.

ZORAN ŽIVKOVIĆ ,
Hidden Camera.

LOUIS ZUKOFSKY,
Collected Fiction.

VITOMIL ZUPAN,
Minuet for Guitar.

SCOTT ZWIREN,
God Head.